"More?" Paul arched
perfect black eyebrows.

Startled, Andrea glanced up and felt her
gaze become entangled in a soft web of
velvet blue. "Ah . . . yes, thank you." In
breathless amazement, she watched
him fill her glass without spilling a drop
or shifting his gaze as much as a flicker
from hers.

"You're welcome." Paul's voice was as
soft and as velvety dark as his eyes.

Andrea's breath eased from her lips
when he released her gaze to return to
his chair. She felt touched in an odd
way, as if his piercing gaze had looked
through the windows of her eyes into
her mind and her heart and her soul.
Shaken, she closed her eyes.

Was she losing touch with reality? But
which reality? she wondered. The reality of nightly dreams of a fantasy lover?
Or the waking reality of the incredible
man seated near her? *Paul was the living image of her nocturnal lover . . .*

Joan Hohl

Joan Hohl, a Gemini and an inveterate day-dreamer, says she always has her head in the clouds. An avid reader all her life, she discovered romances about ten years ago. "And as soon as I read one," she confesses, "I was hooked." Now an extremely prolific author, she is thrilled to be getting paid for doing exactly what she loves best.

Look for *Window on Yesterday* (#450)
and *Window on Today* (#454),
first and second in this magical trilogy!

Dear Reader:

Along with warmer weather and lightening sky, March brings you *Window on Tomorrow* (#458), the third book in Joan Hohl's wonderful trilogy, and classic Second Chance at Love author Carole Buck's *Simply Magic* (#459).

You've met Andrea Trask as a witness to the loves of her roommates in *Window on Yesterday* (#450) and *Window on Today* (#454). Now Andrea faces a love that challenges the tests of time—and place! When Andrea sees her new earth-studies professor, she knows he's perfect, the man of her dreams—literally! But in fact, she's not dreaming. Her fantasy and gorgeous Paul Hellka are one and the same. After class discussions lead to soulful talks and long walks, Andrea finds herself still holding back. Although Paul is as ideal in reality as he was in her fantasies, something's not quite right. There's something mysterious about this dream-come-true that Andrea can't figure out. *Window on Tomorrow* (#458) is an ambitious adventure that will leave you full of wonder.

From the author of *The Real Thing* (#448), *Simply Magic* (#459) introduces a uniquely enticing hero, Dr. Archimedes Xavier "Meade" O'Malley. Awakened by strange music from the apartment below, Brooke Livingstone suddenly believes all the tall tales she's heard about her anthropologist neighbor, Dr. O'Malley. One strange meeting confirms those tales: he's intelligent, eccentric, charming, and handsome. And now he's interested in Brooke. Drawn to him as she is, it's still going to take a lot more than shared interests and spine-tingling passion to capture Brooke's disillusioned heart. Shattered dreams still fresh, Brooke harbors a painful secret. Have no fear—if anyone can show Brooke that time heals all wounds, that true love *is* simply magic, Meade O'Malley can...

Also from Berkley this month is *New York Times* bestselling author Cynthia Freeman's *The Last Princess,* an Alternate Selection of the Literary Guild and a Main Selection of the Doubleday Book Club. Lily had almost everything she desired, and yet, on the eve of her wedding, she threw it all away—for the love of another man. Harry Kohle was everything her parents despised, but Lily knew she couldn't resist Harry's love. From the high society of New York's Upper East Side, to the corrupting glamour of Hollywood, to the haunting beauty of Israel, their love faced the ultimate tests of hardship, struggle, and betrayal.

March also brings a spectacular novel by another *New York Times* bestselling author, LaVyrle Spencer. In the tradition of *Vows* and *The Gamble* is *The Hellion*. They were two loves, two worlds apart. Rachel is at the pinnacle of elegance, social standing, and beauty—when the wildest, most passionate flame of her youth steps into her life again. Tommy Lee's the all-time hell-raiser of Russellville, Alabama, with three marriages behind him and a string of fast cars and women. The townsfolk say he'll never change. But Rachel knows differently. Finally, don't miss *Silk and Satin* by author Marcia Wolfson. It's the story of a simple young woman seduced by the world of the wealthy, who must draw her strength from the one man most dangerous to her—the detective out to prove her guilt in the murder of her millionaire husband. From glass-walled boardrooms and Fire Island hideaways, to East Side watering holes and back room deal makers, *Silk and Satin* holds you in its glamorous grip until the shocking climax!

Don't miss these fabulous offerings—which are sure to chase any remnant chill from winter's weather—from some of the most accomplished writers on the romance scene today.

Until next month, enjoy and...

Happy reading!

Hillary Cige

Hillary Cige, Editor
SECOND CHANCE AT LOVE
The Berkley Publishing Group
200 Madison Avenue
New York, NY 10016

SECOND CHANCE AT LOVE™

JOAN HOHL
WINDOW ON TOMORROW

BERKLEY BOOKS, NEW YORK

WINDOW ON TOMORROW

First edition published March 1989

ISBN: 0-425-11462-7

"Second Chance at Love" and the butterfly emblem are trademarks belonging to Jove Publications, Inc. The name "BERKLEY" and the "B" logo are trademarks belonging to Berkley Publishing Corporation.

Second Chance at Love books are published by
The Berkley Publishing Group
200 Madison Avenue, New York, NY 10016

Printed in the United States of America

10 9 8 7 6 5 4 3 2 1

WINDOW ON TOMORROW

Chapter One

HE WAS THE MOST perfectly beautiful person she had ever seen.

Andrea Trask had never before set eyes on the man in the flesh. And yet she knew him! Literally stunned by the sight of the man, she stared at him through the wide plate-glass window in utter fascination as he approached the coffee shop.

He was exceptionally tall and attractively slender. Though wide, his shoulders didn't have the bunched-muscled look of so many of the young men Andrea had met and observed since arriving in California a few months ago. His hands were broad; his wrists, waist, and hips were narrow. His legs were long and well formed, and he moved with a grace she could only describe as fluid. But it was his face that immediately snared attention, as Andrea noticed from the looks— some furtive, some bold—that he was commanding from everyone, male and female, in the vicinity. His face, the configuration of his classic features, embodied perfection. His wind-tousled, wavy blue-black hair and his bronzed skin gleamed in the bright autumn sunshine. And she knew him.

He stopped on the sidewalk to speak to another man, who had just exited the café. Watching his sculpted lips move, Andrea gasped when a flashing smile revealed his even white teeth. She recognized the smile and responded to it. Without a close look, Andrea knew his eyes were the same shade of blue as a shadowed mountain lake, and were every bit as deep. The knowing, the familiarity she felt, was more than strange—it was downright eerie.

How was it possible? Andrea's rattled mind demanded. It simply wasn't conceivable to suddenly encounter the walking, breathing image of the shade who had invaded her dreams for over a year . . . was it?

Andrea couldn't think, couldn't reason; she could only stare in absolute disbelief.

"Not bad, huh?"

Andrea transferred her gaze with obvious reluctance to the blond young woman seated opposite her in the booth. "Not bad?" she repeated, compulsively shifting her startled gaze to the man again. "Evaluating *him* as 'not bad' is tantamount to judging the Pacific as a large pond!" Andrea's hushed voice revealed her awe.

"Yeah," the blond breathed, nodding in agreement. "The sight of him is rather overpowering." She sighed dramatically. "I don't know how we'll ever concentrate on his lectures."

The remark snagged Andrea's attention. Frowning, she returned her puzzled gaze to the young woman who had become her friend shortly after her arrival in California. "Lectures? Melly, I don't understand. What lectures?"

Melinda Franklin's big brown eyes grew even bigger in surprise. "Didn't you see his photo in the college brochure?" When Andrea shook her head, she explained, "That gorgeous embodiment of every woman's fantasy is none other than Paul Hellka, professor of earth science studies at Parker."

Andrea gaped at her friend, startled as much by her phrasing as by the information she'd imparted. "Fantasy" was exactly what the man was to Andrea. A fantasy, a figment of her imagination, a dream lover—at least, that's what Andrea had believed he was.

Seeing him in the flesh gave Andrea a weird, disoriented sensation. It was too unreal, she assured herself, fighting a clawing sense of panic. It wasn't true. It couldn't be true. The man was merely similar to her dream lover. That was it. Andrea's pulse rate increased with each successive, rationalizing thought. Her brow grew moist; her throat went dry.

"Professor Hellka?" Andrea's voice cracked.

Melinda laughed. "Doesn't look like anyone's idea of a professor, does he?"

Afraid to trust her voice, Andrea again shook her head, but only she knew that the action was also a denial of what she'd seen. Telling herself that all she had to do to ease her shocked mind was look at him again, really look at him, Andrea gritted her teeth and slowly shifted her gaze to the window.

He was gone. The sidewalk in front of the coffee shop was deserted. Had she imagined him? Andrea asked herself. But no, she answered at once. Hadn't Melly told her who he was? Melly! Andrea whipped around to stare at her friend.

"Are you all right?" Melly peered at her with concern. "You look kinda green around the gills."

"Yes! But ... ah, I ..." Andrea raked her numbed mind for an excuse to leave. "I have to go!" she blurted out, groping for her canvas carryall. "I'm really sorry to desert you, Melly, but I just remembered an appointment."

"But you haven't even tasted your lunch!" Melly exclaimed, motioning at the untouched salad in front of Andrea.

Andrea withdrew a couple bills from her bag while sliding out of the booth. "I'm not really hungry," she said, slinging the bag's long strap over her shoulder. "I've got to go. I'll call you later." She took off like a rocket along the line of booths. Near the entrance door, she came to a breathless, jarring halt. He was there, leaning against the back of the first booth, patiently waiting to be seated.

From a distance of only a few feet, Andrea could no longer avoid the truth. He was the living, breathing duplicate of the man in her dreams. Quivering with reactive shock, she hovered on the brink of decision. Should she retreat back to the relative safety of the booth and Melly or go forward to escape by rushing past him?

In the instant Andrea agonized over her choices, he looked directly at her. She had to clamp her lips together to contain a gasp. His eyes were dark, dark blue and were sparked by a perceptive, knowing expression.

"Hello."

The sound of his voice struck Andrea like a physical blow; it was exactly the same as the dream voice she knew so intimately. Reeling from the shock waves washing over her, Andrea mumbled an incoherent greeting, then hurried past him and pushed through the heavy door. She ran to her aunt's car, which she'd parked on the tree-lined street.

Twenty minutes later Andrea parked the dented compact in the driveway of her aunt Celia's home. She had no recollection of the drive along the coast to the house perched on the rock cliffs overlooking the Pacific a few miles south of Carmel. Still clutching the steering wheel, she stared at the house, which was barely visible from the road.

Andrea had fallen in love with the cliff house the minute she entered it the previous spring. At the invitation of her aunt, she had arrived in California the first week of June, exactly two weeks after graduating from college in her home state of Pennsylvania. Andrea's original plan had been to spend a few weeks with her aunt before returning home to Lancaster.

Prying her aching fingers from the wheel, Andrea slumped in the seat. Encountering the walking, talking prototype of her fantasy lover had exhausted her. She felt not quite with-it and a little queasy in her stomach. Getting out of the car and into the house was a physical ordeal.

"Andrea?" Celia Trask called from the patio off the dining room. "Is that you, honey?"

"Yes." Andrea squared her shoulders and worked her lips into a semblance of a smile as she made her way to the patio. A genuine smile eased her stiff mouth at the sight that met her haunted hazel eyes.

Wearing a broad-brimmed straw hat to protect her flawless complexion, and a skimpy bikini that exposed most of her slender, well-toned body to the sun's tanning rays, Celia was stretched out on a padded lounge chair, daintily sipping a frosted glass of mint iced tea. Her oiled honey-browned skin gleamed in the sunlight.

She looked to be somewhere in her mid- to late thirties; she was, in fact, fifty-seven years old. The realization of her aunt's age never failed to amaze Andrea; the fact that she resembled Celia never failed to please her. Thanks to the passage of all the right genes, Andrea possessed the same flawless skin, gentle beauty, and slim, long-limbed suppleness as did her father's sister Celia.

"What's up, sugar?" Celia's voice was soft; her shaded, amber-rimmed hazel eyes were sharp. "I thought you were having lunch with Melinda."

Andrea's smile quirked whimsically at the endearment; Celia was the only person to ever call her sugar. "I was, but . . ." she lifted her shoulders in a small shrug of resignation. She couldn't force herself to lie outright to her aunt, but she couldn't tell her the literal truth, either. Andrea had always admired her aunt for her open mind and free-thinking approach to life, but she doubted that even Celia would understand her niece's present predicament.

"But . . . ?" Celia prompted, probing Andrea's pale face with a laser look.

Andrea sighed. "But I was feeling a bit off center," she explained, opting for the truth . . . as far as she dared.

Swinging her long shapely legs off the lounge, Celia rose and crossed the patio to Andrea. Raising a slim hand, she placed her palm on Andrea's forehead, then slid it to the curve of her throat. "You do feel slightly feverish." Celia frowned. "Perhaps you've contracted a summer virus from one of your customers."

Andrea nodded, quickly grasping the excuse for her unusual behavior. Since she had been working for over a month as a part-time sales clerk in a popular Carmel boutique, the possibility of Andrea having contacted a virus from one of the establishment's many customers was valid. "Perhaps," she conceded, fully aware that the only contact she'd made was with an impossible reality. The awareness drained her face of the little color that remained. Andrea swayed with a sudden light-headedness.

"Andrea!" Alarm gave a discordant note to Celia's musical voice. Grasping Andrea by the arm, she led her inside, out of the glare of sunlight. "I'm putting you to bed," she said, drawing her unresistant niece toward the bedroom. "And then I'm calling the doctor."

"No!" Andrea jarred both herself and her aunt by coming to an abrupt halt. "I'm certain I don't need a doctor, Aunt Celia," she went on in a placating tone, recognizing the look of determination on the older woman's face. "I'll go to bed, but I don't think a doctor will be necessary."

True to character, Celia refused to budge without gaining concessions. "All right, I won't call the doctor," she agreed, but added adamantly, "but I insist you remain in bed until you're feeling completely well, and I intend to call the manager at the boutique and tell her you won't be able to work for a few days." Her expression said clearly that she would brook no argument from Andrea. "Agreed?"

Though Andrea bristled at the thought of confinement, she knew better than to argue with Celia when she was wearing her stubborn look. And she probably knew better because she herself was immovable when she dug her heels in, Andrea acknowledged in silent amusement.

"Okay," she agreed on a sigh. "I promise I'll stay put until I'm in fighting form again." She hesitated, then added a qualifying "I'll stay close to the house, if not actually in it or in my bed."

Smart enough to recognize a will as strong as her own, Celia accepted the compromise with a nod and a rueful laugh. "That will suffice, I suppose." Without indulging in the usual matronly fussing, she stayed with Andrea until she slid between the flower-strewn sheets on her bed. Then she drew the window curtains against the brilliant sunshine and quietly left the room.

Her trembling body stiff, her eyes wide, Andrea lay staring at the dappled pattern of sunlight and shadow filtering through the curtains onto the flat-white wall. She was afraid to close her eyes, afraid to sleep, afraid of . . .

In desperation, Andrea changed the direction of her train of thought. She would not think about *him*! Her mind darted around in a frantic search of a safe point of focus.

Home! That was it. She would think about home; she'd recall her college years and the friends she'd lived with, the apartment they'd shared.

Staring at the wall, but no longer seeing it, Andrea concentrated on conjuring comforting memories. Images swirled in a kaleidoscopic blur inside her mind. Bits and pieces of memories flashed brightly, then faded, to be superseded by other bits and pieces.

Andrea could see herself as a child, laughing as she was swept off her sturdy little legs and into the loving haven of her father's arms. The image changed, and she viewed herself, sobbing and grief-stricken at her father's funeral. A whirl of her mind, and Andrea was reliving the pain of parting with her mother as she watched her board a plane for her new husband's home in South Carolina.

Andrea blinked against a rush of hot tears. The memory still hurt. She had been in her junior year of high school and too involved with her friends and school activities to notice how serious the relationship was becoming between her mother and her new friend. The announcement of their imminent marriage had come as a complete shock to Andrea.

In rapid sequence, images of succeeding events in her young life flashed in painful detail through Andrea's whirling mind.

There in bright clarity was the tearful scene between her and her mother when Andrea had opted to remain in Lancaster to graduate from high school with her friends and classmates.

Then there was the day she had moved in with her mother's sister, Irene, and the homesickness Andrea had suffered, despite her aunt's kindness and caring.

A memory swirl, and Andrea was reliving the thrill she'd experienced when a good-looking, upwardly mobile young businessman had shown an obvious interest in her at a country club dance in the spring of her senior year of high school.

Andrea shook her head in an attempt to dispel the humiliating memory. She didn't want to remember her naiveté and gullibility, but the memory persisted.

The young man's name was Zach, a diminutive of Zaccheus, a biblical name meaning "pure and righteous"—he was neither. Without care or consideration of her age and inexperience, he had swept her off her feet. Before graduation day, Andrea was in love. It was only later, too much later, that she realized Zach was an opportunist. His mode of seduction lacked finesse; Andrea's initiation into womanhood was demeaning and painful. She innocently blamed herself; Zach arrogantly agreed. Playing into his hands, Andrea accepted his scorn without question. She might have continued to play by his rules indefinitely had he not tripped himself up.

To persuade her to live with him, Zach had told Andrea he'd love and protect her forever; he simply forgot to mention who, exactly, would protect her from him. Andrea had been living with him for nearly a year, working part-time at night and attending college classes during the day when, on returning early from work to their small apartment, she found him in a compromising position with another, younger girl. Zach revealed his true character during the argument that followed the girl's ejection from what Andrea had considered her home. For the first time in their relationship, Zach became violent, striking Andrea, then forcing himself on her. It was the first and last time he did either; Andrea made sure of that. She ended their relationship without a twinge of remorse, but with a bitterness far beyond her tender age.

But Zach had the last laugh, and the last blow—at least figuratively. He left Lancaster for greener pastures, and he took Andrea's inheritance from her father with him. Without the inheritance, which she had planned to use for her college expenses, Andrea was forced to leave school. And, though Celia had offered her financial assistance, Andrea had politely but firmly refused the aid, since she had gone against Celia's advice when she had decided to live with Zach. From then on, Andrea had been determined to earn her own way.

She was twenty-four before she managed to save enough money to return to school to complete her education. The intervening years had consisted of working two jobs and doing without not only luxuries but quite often necessities as well.

Recalling the drudgery and self-imposed loneliness of those years brought a fine film of tears to Andrea's eyes. The patterns of shadow and light on the bedroom wall merged, separated, then merged again. Afraid to close her eyes, she stared through the tears and silently prayed for an end to the painful memories.

Whether by divine intervention or sheer willpower, the swirling memories of those difficult years and the echo of Zach's superior laughter dissolved and were replaced by the images and voices of the two young women with whom Andrea had shared an apartment throughout her four-year college sojourn. With a long sigh of relief, Andrea smiled mistily and gratefully allowed remembrances of her friends free rein.

On the surface, they had seemed a mismatched trio. Andrea smiled as the mind-pictures developed into sharper focus.

There was Alycia Halloran *née* Matlock, with her nose in a book—a history book—her gaze focused on yesterday.

And there was Karla Janowitz, meticulously working out the household accounts, her attention and her feet firmly planted in the earth of today.

And there she was, Andrea Trask, the misty-eyed dreamer, her sights set on the possibilities of tomorrow.

A mismatched trio? Perhaps. But it had been circumstances, not common interests, that had drawn them together.

Her memory unwinding, Andrea forgot her fears. Her eyelids grew heavy, then slowly drifted downward. Defying time, her memory spun back four years.

* * *

"Are you alone?"

At the sound of the gently voiced question, Andrea glanced up from the rooms-for-rent section of the local newspaper. An attractive young woman gazed down at her, a hopeful light reflecting from her soft eyes.

"Yes," Andrea answered. "Would you like to join me?" she asked, glancing around. The Campus Café was packed with young people. Laughter and chattering conversation reverberated off the poster-plastered walls. There wasn't a seat to be had—except in the booth Andrea occupied.

The woman's sigh was audible. "If you don't mind?" she asked, hesitating before sliding onto the bench seat.

"Be my guest." Andrea smiled and waved her hand at the opposite seat in invitation.

Expelling a pent-up breath, the dark-haired girl slid into the booth with obvious gratitude. "Hi," she said, extending her hand across the table. "I'm Alycia Matlock, and I'm dying for a cup of coffee!"

Andrea laughed in understanding and grasped the proffered hand. "Hi. I'm Andrea—" That was as far as she got when another feminine voice interrupted.

"Is anyone sitting here?"

Startled by the directness of the coolly voiced query, Andrea and Alycia drew their hands back and looked up. The woman standing beside the booth was about their age, beautiful, and, at that moment, obviously out of patience. Andrea repeated her flicked-hand invitation.

"Just us," she replied. "You might as well bring the number to three." Andrea grinned. "I'm Porthos."

"I'm Athos," Alycia chimed in.

"I'm bushed."

There was a heartbeat of silence as the three women

gazed at one another. Then they burst into spontaneous laughter.

"Sorry if I sounded rude," the third woman said when the laughter had subsided. "I'm Karla Janowitz," she continued, offering her hand to each as Andrea and Alycia introduced themselves. "And I really am beat . . . bordering on depressed."

Alycia nodded sagely. "It's going around."

"I think I've been exposed to the virus." Andrea sighed.

The spontaneous laughter erupted again.

"What do you think the chances are of getting waited on in this crush?" Karla wondered aloud when their amusement again died down.

"Slim," Alycia began.

"To none," Andrea finished.

"But I'm parched!" Karla groaned, slumping against the back of the booth. "I've been pounding the pavement all day looking for a room."

"A cubicle," Alycia inserted.

"A closet," Andrea concluded.

"You, too, huh?" Karla shifted her gaze from Alycia to Andrea, then slowly shook her head. "I suppose I should've bypassed independence and gone directly for on-campus housing."

"The same thought occurred to me," Alycia confessed.

"Ditto."

Karla and Alycia stared at Andrea, and then all three again broke into tired laughter.

"You know, if I were a witness to this little scene," Karla observed a moment later, "I'd deduce that the three of us were doing an impression of an old Marx Brothers comedy routine."

"It beats sobbing all over the table," Andrea replied. "Sobbing is so . . . so . . ."

"Immature?" Alycia interjected.

"Yeah."

"Right."

"But I must admit," Alycia went on, nodding at her two companions, "I do feel like wailing right now. How . . . *how*, I ask you, did I ever convince myself that finding a room would be a snap?"

"Don't ask me!" Karla yelped. "I'm rowing the same boat."

"With one oar in the water," Andrea agreed glumly.

"One oar is an apt description." Karla grimaced. "Do you know what I actually did?" Without waiting for a response, she proceeded to tell them. "I actually made an appointment to look at an apartment! I mean, am I getting flaky or what? Hell, on my savings, I can't afford to maintain a small bachelor unit, never mind a three-bedroom apartment!"

"Three bedrooms?" Andrea leaned forward, her expression alert.

Alycia perked up. "You made an appointment?"

Karla didn't disappoint them by being slow on the uptake. "Do you think we could swing it?" she asked, hopefully.

"If we set our hearts and minds to it," Alycia said, her voice soft with yearning.

The two girls regarded Andrea across the narrow booth table. Andrea smiled, then shrugged. "I think the arrangement will work."

It did. The friendship that was forged between the three women that day not only endured through four years of college, but grew into a bond as strong as any shared by the closest of sisters.

Memories flickered through Andrea's mind like the ruffled pages of a book. Laughing times, somber times, scrimping end-of-the-month macaroni-and-cheese-three-nights-a-week times. The memory pages grew fewer in number and more vivid. Memories of the previous spring and the events that broke up the mismatched trio, physically if not emotionally.

Andrea moved restlessly on the bed as she relived the fear and anxiety she and Karla had shared on learning that Alycia had been injured in an automobile accident while driving to Williamsburg during the college spring break.

Then the memory page turned, and Andrea relaxed with a relieved sigh. She and Karla had laughed and cried and hugged each other on receiving the news that Alycia was at last fully conscious after nearly a month of drifting close to the dangerous edge of coma. They rejoiced when Alycia was brought home from the hospital by the drawn but obviously relieved Sean Halloran, the man Alycia had fallen headlong in love with a mere week before the start of spring break.

A soft smile curved Andrea's lips as she recalled the incredible story Alycia had seemed compelled to relate to her and Karla soon after returning home.

While drifting in and out of consciousness as she lay in a hospital bed in Richmond, Virginia, Alycia had felt herself caught in some sort of time warp, transposed in spirit to eighteenth-century Williamsburg. And as if that alone wasn't weird enough, Alycia claimed to have met a man—an eighteenth-century man, no less—who was an officer of the Virginia Rangers, attached to General Washington's staff, and the breathing image of Sean Halloran. The man's name was Patrick Halloran. Alycia further maintained that, quite naturally, she fell in love with Patrick and he with her. But they were forced to part when Patrick's duty leave was over, and Alicia was forced to await news of the battle he was heading into, and whose outcome she already knew. The battle was engaged at Brandywine Creek.

Much agitated, and in wide-eyed seriousness, Alycia had told Andrea and Karla that news eventually reached Williamsburg of Washington's defeat at Brandywine and his subsequent retreat to Valley Forge. Notice was also received of the death of Major Patrick Halloran. Tears had brightened Alycia's horror-filled eyes as she recounted her grief to Andrea and Karla. And tears had overflowed Andrea's eyes as she heard and identified with the pain in Alycia's voice.

"I couldn't believe that fate would be so cruel as to allow me to love and lose the same man, not once but twice. I was wild with grief. Late that night I crept out of the house and saddled a horse, determined to find Patrick, or his grave. I could not get to Sean. I had left him in the future. But I knew how to get to Brandywine. I had to find Patrick!" Alycia's eyes were wide, but looking in, not out. "I rode through the night, hours, hours. There was a storm. The horse bolted and plunged into the forest bordering the road. I struck my head on a low-hanging branch and was thrown from the saddle. I screamed for Sean, for Patrick. When I awoke, I was in the hospital in Richmond. And Sean was there, holding me close, holding on to me as if he'd fight the devil before letting me go."

Karla, the earthbound realist, had remained skeptical throughout the retelling of the strange experience. When Alycia finished on a cry of "Did it happen or was it all a hallucinatory dream?" Karla relented enough to offer words of assurance; but even those were thinly veiled with cynicism.

"Of course it was a dream, Alycia. A very under-standable dream. You had been studying the Battle of Brandywine Creek for weeks before you left for Williamsburg. In addition, dare I remind you that you met and fell in love with Sean a week before your departure? You suffered a head injury in the accident." Her smile held a hint of superiority that had become endearingly familiar to both her friends. "I can see that the dream would seem very real to you, under the circumstances. But I'm positive that it was only a dream."

Deeply moved and oddly affected by the tale, Andrea wasn't nearly as certain as Karla appeared to be. "I don't know," she said softly, unashamedly brushing the tears from her cheeks while grasping Alycia's hand tightly with her other hand. "Come to that," she went on more strongly when Karla snorted, "who actually does know whether or not it's possible to travel through time on some sort of warp?"

"I give up!" Karla rolled her eyes in exasperation and turned to walk to the door. But she paused in the door-way to grin at them over her shoulder. "It's a good thing I genuinely love you two," she said wryly. "Because you both really are eccentric yo-yos, you know." Then she was gone, her soft, indulgent laughter wafting back to them from the stairway.

The memory of Karla's achingly familiar laughter echoed inside Andrea's head, bringing a sleepy smile to her lips. Images flickered and flared, and her smile soft-ened as the resonant echo of laughter became the voices of Alycia and Sean on the glorious May morning they exchanged vows of marriage.

The mismatched trio had split to go their separate ways. A few hours after their wedding ceremony, Aly-cia and Sean drove away from the apartment amid a

shower of laughter and birdseed, headed for an undis-
closed honeymoon destination. Before the end of the
following week, Andrea and Karla had finished packing
their things and cleaning the apartment. Emotions running close to the surface, and unabashed tears streaking
their mascara, they parted company, Karla to Sedona,
Arizona, and the art gallery she'd plunged herself into
debt to establish, and Andrea to her aunt Irene's home
in Lancaster, to anxiously await a response to her appli-
cation for employment with NASA.

The letter of rejection arrived from Houston one
week after Andrea returned to Lancaster, and one day
before the letter of invitation arrived from her aunt
Celia.

At loose ends, unemployed, and feeling more than
ever like a stranger in her aunt Irene's home, Andrea
had accepted Celia's invitation at once. Near the end of
the initial two-week visit, Celia had extended the invitation, generously leaving it open-ended. And now the
summer was nearly over, and Andrea was working with
a whole new set of plans. She had taken a part-time job
and had enrolled for post-graduate classes in a local college that was quite small but highly accredited.

Memory was beginning to blur and dissolve in the
mist of advancing sleep. Yet, even cocooned in the
nether world of half-sleep, Andrea felt a pang of regret.
She had geared her studies toward aeronautics and had
looked forward so eagerly to working in some capacity
with the NASA team planning future space probes.

A soft sigh whispered from her throat. All but one of
the memory pages and echoes were gone. And the one
remaining page was the single memory Andrea had
hoped to avoid. Her hope was shattered by the weakness
induced by encroaching sleep.

The memory spanned an entire year. At times lonely for male companionship, yet afraid to trust another man, Andrea had dreamed up a fantasy lover, a man unlike other men, perfect in appearance and character. At times her dreams had seemed every bit as real as Alycia's experience seemed to her, but Andrea had never, ever considered the possibility of someday meeting her fantasy lover while she was wide awake.

And yet she had seen him today with her own eyes, had registered his appearance with her fully conscious mind, had been given his name by her friend.

It wasn't possible! Moaning softly, Andrea struggled against surrendering to the shadowy wisps of sleep. But her struggles were weak, and she lost the battle. Reality retreated before the billowing darkness of slumber. She was floating, cushioned by the cloud of unconsciousness. There was a hazy form in the distance, moving toward her with long, leisurely strides. The form took on substance as it drew nearer. He was very tall and incredibly, unbelievably handsome. His smile struck a light in her soul. His voice was a soft caress in her heart.

"Hi, sugar."

Chapter Two

HE HELD OUT HIS hand to her. Unafraid, she entwined her fingers with his.

In slumber Andrea knew him. They had met like this throughout a year of nightly dreams. It was always the same; he came to her out of the mist of sleep clouding her mind. He held out his hand; she gave him hers. Every dream had begun exactly the same. This one was different.

He had called her "sugar."

Andrea knew she was dreaming. The conscious part of her mind, still attuned to reality, registered a vague sense of alarm. Why had he used that particular endearment?

As in all previous dreams, he turned toward a narrow grass-bordered path.

The sense of unease expanded within the reality-oriented part of Andrea, and for the first time, she resisted being drawn completely into the dream. Fighting the allure of him and the path along which he would lead her, she struggled to wake up.

But the sleeping part of Andrea had a mind of her own. Setting her sable-dark hair swirling with an impatient toss of her head, she clasped his hand tightly, as if to anchor herself in his domain, and stepped onto the path beside him.

Looking past her sleeping self, he smiled with gentle understanding at Andrea's conscious, resistant self. His eyes held the glow of ancient wisdom.

"Come along. You know you want to." His voice was soft, tender, coaxing. "Give in to the longing and need and desire you conceal so well."

While her sleeping self stood mute, waiting, Andrea's earthly, conscious self fought an inner battle. She was afraid, afraid of losing herself; but she yearned to go, to lose herself with him, in him. The inner conflict was fierce between unconscious desires and the fear of disassociation.

He ended her internal war by murmuring one word that was at once a request, a plea, and a command.

"Come."

Unequal to the strength of her own unleashed needs, Andrea divorced herself from consciousness and merged with the essence of her own unconscious, sleeping self.

The dreamscape changed immediately. The shadowed mist evaporated in the sparkling sunlight. The scene was familiar to Andrea. She recognized the rough, tree-dotted terrain and the path that was just wide enough to allow her to walk beside him.

In shade-dappled sunshine, they strolled hand in hand to a small grass-cushioned clearing beneath the wind-twisted branches of a large old tree. Pulling An-

drea down with him, he dropped to the ground. He settled his back against the age-gnarled tree trunk, then
drew her slender form into the embracing cradle of his
parted thighs.

Exhaling a sigh of utter contentment, Andrea snug-
gled into the haven of his warm body and rested her
head on the pillow of his chest.

"Are you now glad you gave in?" His breath ruffled
the hair at the crown of her head; his nearness ruffled
her senses.

"Yes."

"And are you now happy?" His voice held a hint of
amusement, as though he knew what her answer would
be.

Andrea didn't mind at all—in fact, she shared his
amusement. "Oh, yes!"

"Then I'm happy, too."

They were quiet for a time, content to bask in their
mutual inner emotional rhythms. Andrea could hear the
music of a restless sea in the background. She had heard
and identified the sound during the very first dream of
him, yet in over a year she had never actually seen the
source of the ocean song. The dream always opened in
the mist at the beginning of the path and ended in that
grass-padded spot beneath the old tree in the clearing.

In her waking hours, Andrea carried in a guarded
section of her heart and mind the memory of the tree,
the clearing, the sound of a distant sea, and him. She
had learned to know him in this secret place, had come
to the realization that he was the representation of her
ideal of male perfection. They had held long conversa-
tions in this shaded bower. They had laughed freely together.

During the winter months of strung-together dreams,

Andrea had come to trust him. And through that trust, and because her accumulated dreams slowly began to seem more real to Andrea than waking reality, she had come to love him. Inevitably, as her love for him grew and deepened, it added a new, anticipatory dimension to her dreams.

His ultimate possession of her became the stuff of her unconscious and conscious longings. While going about her daily routine, presenting to her friends and acquaintances the Andrea they believed they knew, she lived for the nights, for the precious moments spent with him, secretly longing for his ultimate possession of her dream self.

Strangely, though her dreams became more erotic and his caresses grew nightly more arousing, he had never crossed that final barrier, had never fulfilled the longing that consumed her thoughts, waking or sleeping.

Now, her waking conscious submerged within the dream state, Andrea expressed all her longing in a soft sigh.

"Andrea?" His long, elegant fingers brushed the length of her thigh in a feather-light stroke.

"Hmm?" She responded to his caress by moving sensuously against him.

"Why do you sigh, my heart?" His stroking fingers explored the curving outline of her form from her rounded hip to her shoulder; his fingers gently probed the hollow at the base of her throat.

Andrea smiled and rubbed her cheek against the back of his hand. He had begun calling her "my heart" on the night of her arrival in California. Delighted with the endearment, Andrea had raised her mouth to his, initiating the love play between them. He had rewarded her bravery by breathing the endearment into her mouth. Would he reward her again if she confessed to the reason for her sigh?

Temptation beckoned, and after a moment's uncertainty, Andrea surrendered to it. "I love you," she whispered.

His fingers encircled her arched throat; his voice was a low siren song of enticement against her ear. "And loving me causes you to sigh?"

Andrea searched for a way to explain, a way to tell him of her secret longing to be one with him. In desperation she cried, "I don't even know your name!"

"My name is love," he murmured, gliding his lips to her mouth. "*Your* love."

Enlightenment washed over Andrea's clouded senses. Of course! She had created him, weaving her fantasy out of the threads of her loneliness and longing. He was hers exclusively. He was hers to command.

"My love." Andrea breathed, testing the sound of his name on her voice.

"Yes." He brushed his mouth over hers. "Only two words are required, my heart. Say the words and I'll open the door to paradise for you." His voice went low, almost nonexistent. "Say the words."

There was no doubt, no question in Andrea's mind. She knew the magic words; she didn't hesitate to use them or to add two alluring words of her own.

"Love me, my love."

There were no awkward moments, no embarrassed fumbling with undressing. Since her dream world was not governed by the constricting laws of physical reality, the material of convention disappeared from their bodies. Within an instant of dream time, Andrea found herself lying beside him in the grassy bower, thrilling to the exciting new sensation of feeling his naked skin glide sensuously over hers.

There was a subtle difference in his caress; the difference made Andrea's senses take fire. His hands stroked her quivering body with a gentleness bordering on reverence. Each touch, each stroke, each caress, fed the flames leaping along her quivering nerve endings. The ethereal lightness of his touch teased her senses to an unbearable height.

In contrast, his mouth and tongue plundered the sweetness of hers with bold audacity. His lips were cool and firm, his kiss was hot and wet, enveloping her, taking, giving. Raking, plunging, caressing, the evocative play of his thrusting tongue drove her over the edge of compliance and into the role of aggressor.

The clawing demand for unity in the deepest part of her femininity sent her hands to his hips to guide his body into the embrace of her thighs.

Mirroring her motion, he glided his long hands from her aching breasts to her arching hips. His bottomless blue eyes held her gaze captive as he slid his hands beneath her, lifting her up into the forward thrust of his body.

Andrea cried out her pleasure at the instant of his exquisite entrance into her body.

Penetration. Possession. Union.

Her shudder was reflected in and absorbed by his own.

They were one; she a part of him; he a part of her.

He paused, allowing them both sweet seconds to savor the oneness of their separate beings. Then, slowly, he began to move. Moaning and trembling from the magnitude of sensations swirling through her, Andrea clung to his taut flanks, her fingers flexing, her nails driving him deeper and ever deeper into the very heart of her passion.

Tension.

Andrea had never before experienced the power of the tension winding tightly inside her body. It expanded, blossomed, devoured her muscles, her nerves, her mind. Andrea pleaded for it to end . . . and begged for it to go on forever.

When the tension snapped, the whiplash launched her into a universe of exploding feelings and sensations and brilliant, blinding colors.

Paradise.

The exultant sound of his beloved voice calling her name was the last sound she heard.

Andrea lost all form of consciousness.

She woke again to the dream. Her love was with her, inside her, part of her. The gentle breeze caressed their joined bodies; the distant sea sang a lovers' serenade.

"I love you." Andrea stroked his silky, sweat-dampened hair with trembling fingers.

"I know." He raised his head from her breast to smile into her passion-shaded eyes, "As I knew that only together was the attainment of perfection possible."

"Yes." In that instant, Andrea realized that only with him could she glimpse paradise.

"Yes." His eyes were soft with understanding, as if he'd heard her thoughts.

"Please." Her whisper revealed the ache in her soul. "Love me back."

"I do." His smile held infinite tenderness. "I always have."

"Always?" Her smile was uncertain.

"Always." His smile grew serious. "From the moment of your creation."

Her creation? Andrea frowned. Surely he meant from the moment she had created him in her mind? "But . . ." His patient, understanding expression stole the words from her throat and brought a question to her lips. "My love?"

"Yes," he whispered. "Always your love."

Andrea didn't understand; but then, it really didn't matter. She sighed with contentment. Her sigh changed to a murmured protest when he withdrew from her.

"I am here," he said, drawing her into the haven of his arms. "You are safe."

Until morning. The thought opened up a fissure of unease in Andrea; the rift separated her from her unconscious self. Morning meant waking, and waking meant facing . . . Andrea shuddered as memory flooded her consciousness.

"Andrea?"

Andrea heard his voice with her conscious and unconscious selves. And his voice was the same as that of the man she had seen in the flesh at the coffee shop. Deep inside, Andrea knew that her wish for his possession had been the reason for her flight from his physical duplicate earlier that day.

The intrusion of earthly concerns into the mind of her sleeping self made Andrea uneasy. She transmitted her discomfort to him by moving against him restlessly.

"Tell me."

He didn't have to elaborate; she understood. He had conveyed a depth of meaning and compassion with those two softly spoken words.

"I saw your physical image today." As she answered, Andrea twisted around in his embrace to catch whatever expression he might reveal.

His smile was tender and enigmatic. "And the sight

upset you?" He trailed his fingers from her wrist to her shoulder in a feather-light caress.

Andrea gasped, amazed at the intensity of the thrill that tingled through her. "I . . . I was shocked," she admitted on an indrawn breath. "I never expected to actually see anyone who even vaguely resembled you. But to see your mirror image! And then to learn that that person is the professor of one of the classes I'd planned to attend this fall!"

"Planned to attend?" He didn't raise his voice or lose his smile. "You've now changed your mind about attending the classes?"

Until that instant, Andrea hadn't been aware of having changed her mind, but in the murky depths of her gray matter, she had decided to withdraw from the course.

"It's unnecessary, you know." His bottomless blue eyes held the gleam of secret amusement.

Andrea blinked in astonishment; he had reassured her before she had told him of her decision! Could he read her unconscious mind? "It's . . . it's not?" she responded in a dry croak.

His eyes and smile were tender. "No, Andrea. You have nothing to fear from Paul Hellka."

He knew the professor's name! How? Suddenly frightened, Andrea scrambled up and began running along the path, back to reality and the safety of her conscious self. She felt a pang in her chest when he called her name.

"Andrea!"

Andrea jolted upright on the bed. Her eyes were wide and moist with tears.

"Andrea, wake up!" Celia called.

Andrea blinked. Her aunt was sitting on the edge of

the bed, stroking Andrea's arm, the same arm *he* had stroked. "Wh . . . what's wrong?" Andrea's throat felt stuffed with cotton. "Is something wrong?"

"No, nothing," Celia said soothingly. "You're all right, sugar. It was only a dream."

Only a dream! A tremor ripped through Andrea; her fingers flexed and curled into her palm. Only a dream. Her love. Their lovemaking . . . Only a dream? Fighting an urge to laugh and cry hysterically at the same time, she stared into Celia's concern-darkened eyes.

"What time is it?" Andrea was amazed that she sounded so normal; she felt anything but normal.

"It's not quite six," Celia answered, narrowing her eyes as she examined Andrea's face. "You're not as pale as you were. Are you feeling better?"

The question startled Andrea, until she remembered the reason she had been sleeping in the middle of the day. Not quite six! She had returned to the house around one! Still slightly disoriented by the sudden transition from the dream world to reality, Andrea had to concentrate to determine exactly how she did feel.

Her smile was faint. "I think so, but I'm not sure yet." She shrugged. "I'm not fully awake."

"Are you hungry?"

Was she? Andrea frowned as she contemplated the question. A hollow sensation in her midsection provided the answer. "Yes, I am!" she exclaimed in surprise.

Celia heaved an audible sigh of relief. "Good." She patted Andrea's hand as she stood up. "Dinner will be ready in a few minutes." She paused in the doorway to smile back at Andrea. "You have time for a shower . . . if you want one."

"I do." From somewhere, Andrea produced a real smile. "Thanks, Aunt Celia."

The older woman laughed. "For what?"

Andrea's eyes misted over. "Just for being my aunt Celia," she answered in a husky voice.

Celia's expressive eyes, which were so very similar to Andrea's, revealed the pleasure she was feeling. "There are times when I feel more like your mother than your aunt," she said in an emotion-clogged voice. "And many more times that I wish I were." She sniffed, then laughed as she shook her head with impatience. "Now, you have your shower, while I put the finishing touches on dinner." She turned away, but called back over her shoulder, "If you hurry, you can toss the salad."

Burying the clinging remnants of the exciting yet disturbing dream in a secret corner of her mind, Andrea got up, then smoothed the revealingly rumpled bed before heading for the bathroom.

Assisted by Celia's animated chatter, Andrea managed to keep the memory and portent of her dream at bay through dinner. But her memory was jogged in a different direction while they were clearing away the last of the dishes.

"Aunt Celia!" Andrea exclaimed in chagrin. "Didn't you plan to have dinner with Blaine this evening?"

"Yes," Celia replied in an unruffled tone, not glancing up as she carefully stacked dishes into the dishwasher. "But I didn't want to leave you here alone, so I called him and begged off."

"Oh, I'm sorry," Andrea murmured contritely.

Straightening, Celia gave her niece a wry look. "It's not the end of the world, you know." Her lips curved into a droll smile. "As a matter of fact, Blaine was delighted, though he did attempt to hide it."

Andrea found her aunt's remark hard to believe; it had been blatantly obvious from the day she met him that Blaine Parker was besotted by Celia Trask. "Indeed?" she said, giving her aunt a skeptical smile.

"Yes, indeed. So you can stop feeling guilty." Celia smiled serenely. "You see, my call to Blaine came at a propitious moment for him." Her smile indulgent, Celia walked to a corner cabinet and took out an emerald-green bottle. "Put this in the fridge to chill, please," she said, handing the bottle to Andrea.

"I don't understand." Andrea absently stashed the wine in the refrigerator. "And I can't imagine Blaine being delighted about having you break a date." Frowning, she shifted her perplexed eyes from the fridge to her aunt. "And why are you chilling wine *after* dinner?"

Celia's musical laughter danced on the soft evening air. "Let me clear this up for you," she said, crossing the room to Andrea. "Blaine was delighted when I broke our date because a friend of his returned to town unexpectedly today, and Blaine wanted to have dinner with him." Slipping an arm around Andrea's waist, Celia led her from the kitchen to the patio. "And I'm chilling the wine because Blaine said he'd bring his friend here to meet you after dinner." She gave Andrea a brief hug before releasing her and sinking onto a deck chair. "Any other questions?"

"One," Andrea said, frowning as she glanced down at herself. Never even thinking of the prospect of company that evening, she had dressed in sandals, a handkerchief-soft paisley skirt, and a hot pink T-shirt. "Am I presentable?"

Celia looked startled for an instant, then nearly choked on a burst of laughter. "Presentable! Sugar, with your looks and figure, you'd appear presentable decked out in a gunny sack!" She waved her hand in a gesture inclusive of Andrea's face and form. "All I can say is,

I'm glad Blaine seems immune to your appeal . . . even though he obviously appreciates it. As for his friend"— she shrugged and grinned—"he'll have to fend for himself."

Andrea felt a warm tide of pleasure spread over her cheeks. In all honesty, and without conceit, she gratefully acknowledged the feminine appeal of her good looks and slender form. Her attributes were inherited, of course, primarily from the woman gazing at her from eyes bright with pride and love.

"I don't know about the other man," Andrea said, "but I believe that Blaine's immunity to the attractions of other females stems from his deep feelings for you." Her soft laughter floated on the sea-scented breeze. "I mean, even a thoroughly insensitive person couldn't help noticing that Blaine is very much in love with you."

"Hmm, yes, he doesn't even make a show of hiding the way he feels about me." Celia's voice was low and held a faraway, dreamy note. "But then, I'm rather mad about him, too." Settling into the padded lounge, she smiled and closed her eyes, lost for the moment in a reverie of the man she loved.

Walking to the end of the patio, Andrea trailed her hand along the smooth wooden rail and stared out over the moon-gilded Pacific. She paused at the top of the three shallow steps that led down to a small enclosed garden, a soft smile curving her mouth as she glanced back at her aunt.

Convinced by Celia's dreamy expression that she wouldn't be missed for a few minutes, and feeling the need for some exercise after spending the entire afternoon in bed, Andrea descended the steps.

The small garden was anything but formal. Reflecting Celia's personality, the enclosure was neat without being fussy, well planned without being rigid, and a tribute to the abundance of nature without being unbridled.

Lulled by the rhythmic swish of the calm sea, Andrea strolled the narrow pebbled path and contemplated the charming woman who had welcomed her into her home and life with open, loving arms.

In Andrea's opinion, her beloved aunt was one of a kind.

Celia Trask had never married, but she had known love. Soon after moving from Pennsylvania to California to further her career in the then relatively new field of computers, Celia had fallen in love with a married man. The man was handsome, moody, and brilliant. But though he returned Celia's love, he felt morally as well as legally bound to the mother of his two young children.

Since her own upbringing had instilled in her a deep loyalty to moral principles, Celia understood and respected the man's position. Even so, her love had remained unshakable. For twenty-two years Celia had worked with him, laughed with him, loved him. Their love was never consummated . . . it simply existed.

Celia's faith in the man was so strong that, early in their association, she had invested every dollar she possessed and was able to borrow on his breakthrough invention of a small, affordable personal computer. The heavy investment of faith had eventually made her an independently wealthy woman.

But Celia had continued to work as his assistant in the small company that almost overnight became a very large company, until his death four years ago. Then, with her friend, mentor, and spiritual mate gone, Celia had left Silicon Valley and retired to her hideaway house nestled in the craggy hills above the shoreline south of Carmel.

Celia's hideaway hadn't been successful in hiding her from the advances of Blaine Parker.

Andrea laughed aloud at the thought. She had liked the tall, urbane man the moment Celia introduced her to him on the evening Andrea arrived on the West Coast.

Rugged, rangy, and laconic, Blaine did not fit the accepted definition of handsome, nor did he look like anyone's idea of an academician. And yet, as the president of the small but prestigious Parker College—the institution that bore his grandfather's name, as well as his own—that was precisely what Blaine was.

From reading between the lines of the sketchy account her aunt had related to her, Andrea had deduced that Blaine was an academician with the tenacity of a bulldog.

Andrea had further surmised that, after noticing Celia in a restaurant in Carmel the previous fall, Blaine had asked a mutual friend to introduce him to the serenely beautiful Celia and before the introductions were concluded, she had caught his fancy as well as his interest.

Blaine had told Andrea that, for him at least, it was love at first meeting. That meeting obviously didn't have quite the same impact on Celia.

Still true to the memory of the one and only man she had ever loved, Celia had dismissed all thought of Blaine the instant he was out of sight. But Blaine proved difficult to dismiss.

Celia had laughingly told her niece of how she had attempted to dodge Blaine's dogged pursuit of her. Then, after weeks of calling her, writing to her, and actually trailing after her like a lovesick puppy, Blaine had finally succeeded in capturing Celia's attention and, eventually, her affection.

A shiver rippled the length of Andrea's spine as she recalled the note of wonder in her aunt's voice when Celia confessed that she had never really believed in the power of physical love until Blaine had demonstrated it to her. The shiver intensified as the echo of Celia's voice rang inside Andrea's head.

"It was like dying and being born anew, at one and the same time."

At the time, Andrea had silently rejected her aunt's description. She had lived with a man, yet not once had she been inspired with feelings other than embarrassment, shame, and disappointment in connection with the physical act supposedly expressing love.

Now, since her dream experience of that afternoon, Andrea had a mind-altering frame of reference and a deep, spiritual understanding of Celia's assertion. Or did she? she wondered. Her experience had been, after all, only a dream.

Only a dream.

The sound of the murmuring sea filling her mind, Andrea yearned for slumber, and her love.

Only a dream?

A chill shivered along Andrea's spine. Wrapping her arms around her body to contain the shiver, she turned back along the path. But if it *was* only a dream, she reminded herself, she had only to go to sleep to repeat it. Her spirits brightened; the shiver intensified, but for a different reason.

He had said, "Always." Her love had said . . . Andrea's thoughts were scattered by the night-slicing beams of light from the car that drove into the driveway.

Celia's guests had arrived.

Quickening her pace, Andrea shrugged off speculation and strode along the path. She was mounting the steps when the doorbell rang. She heard Blaine's voice as she crossed the patio. The familiar sound of another male voice brought her to a dead stop at the open patio doors. Her eyes wide and haunted, Andrea stared into the face of her fantasy lover, the man who inhabited her dreams.

Chapter Three

HIS EYES SEEMED TO pierce into her soul.

Feeling oddly suspended in space and time, Andrea stood as if rooted to the floor. The moment went on forever, and was over in an instant.

The scene had absolute clarity within that isolated instant; Andrea's senses seemed finely tuned; her vision was sharp, her hearing acute.

She saw the easy camaraderie between Celia, Blaine, and the other man, heard distinctly each word of the warm greetings they exchanged. And yet her attention was riveted on the stranger who was no stranger in another reality.

The resemblance was too complete to be believed.

The man Andrea knew to be professor Paul Hellka was the living, breathing, laughing image of her fantasy lover.

He was exceptionally tall, appealingly slender, and

handsome to the unbelievable point of beautiful. Even his attire was similar to the clothes worn by her dream man.

His narrow waist and hips and his long, well-formed legs were clearly revealed by tight, distressed jeans. A fine-knit V-neck pullover hugged the breadth of his shoulders and afforded a tantalizing peek at the swirling silky black hair on his chest. Expensive but beat-up running shoes completed his casual summertime ensemble.

His longish, windswept, loosely curling black hair had obviously not felt the busy end of a brush since Andrea had seen him earlier that day. His incredible blue eyes had the look of having seen everything.

And he saw Andrea an eternity before either of the others noticed her.

"Ah, there you are, Andrea," Blaine called when he spotted her in the doorway. "Come meet my friend."

Pulling her jangling senses together, Andrea forced her quivering legs to carry her into the living room. She somehow even managed a weak smile for Blaine.

"I'd like you to meet Dr. Paul Hellka," Blaine said. "Paul, this is the young woman I was telling you about. Celia's niece, Andrea Trask."

Doctor? Andrea reflected, shifting her reluctant gaze to the professor. Doctor of what?

"It's a pleasure, Ms. Trask."

The sound of his voice reverberated through her entire being. How could it be? she cried in silent protest. How was it possible that his voice was exactly the same as that of the man she'd created out of loneliness? Feeling strange, unreal, Andrea reached out to accept the hand he offered.

"Dr. Hellka," she responded in a dry-mouthed whisper. The touch of his palm against hers instilled a surge

of conflicting sensations inside Andrea; in an inexplicable way she felt both soothed and wildly agitated.
Withdrawing her hand in a natural manner required
every ounce of control she possessed.

His smile was mesmerizing. "I'd be pleased if you'd
call me Paul."

"If you like . . . Paul," Andrea murmured after a moment of uncertain hesitation. "And please call me Andrea." As she spoke, she raised her eyes to his and was
immediately adrift in a sea of deepest blue. The sound
of her aunt's voice was the lifeline that kept her from
drowning.

"The evening is much too beautiful to stay inside,"
Celia said, motioning with a slim hand. "Why don't you
show Paul out to the patio, sugar, while Blaine and I get
the wine and glasses?"

Blinking herself out of the enticement of midnight
blue, Andrea drew a breath and turned toward the sliding glass doors. "Of course." She paused to moisten her
parched lips. "This way, Dr.—Paul." Without looking
to see if he was following her, she made a beeline for
the doorway.

Andrea's flight ended at the patio railing. She was
trembling inside and shivering on the surface. Her
breathing was shallow and erratic. Though he didn't
make a sound, she sensed him, felt him, an instant before he came to a stop beside her.

"Sugar." His whisper blended with the balmy late
summer breeze. The nearly soundless murmur had the
jarring effect of a shout on Andrea.

"What?" She jolted around to stare at him.

Paul smiled; Andrea bit back a sigh.

"The endearment your aunt used," he explained in a
velvet-soft tone. "Sugar. I like it."

"Do . . . do you?" Her own voice held little substance.

"Yes."

Fighting the disorienting sense of unreality, Andrea strove for a note of normalcy. "Aunt Celia is the only person who calls me that." Even as she made the statement, Andrea heard the echo of a man's voice, *his* voice, saying, "Hi, sugar." Afraid of betraying the tremor the echo caused inside her, she turned to gaze sightlessly at the shimmering ocean.

"Are you cold?" he asked softly, letting her know her ploy had been unsuccessful.

"No!" she denied forcefully, much too forcefully. "I . . . er, no," Andrea said in a calmer tone. "I'm not at all cold." To herself she admitted that she was chilled from shock and disbelief, and from an insidious fear that she might be losing her mind.

"Andrea."

Andrea stiffened; her heart skipped a beat. Paul's voice had the exact intonation as . . . No! She clamped down on the thought. It wasn't possible; all of her intellect and reason told her it simply was not possible for Paul and her fantasy man to be one and the same. The very concept was too bizarre, too far out to be contemplated.

"Yes?" Hanging on to the patio rail for support, Andrea turned her head to look at him.

His smile stole her breath and the small amount of sense she'd had left. "I understand that you've enrolled in my earth studies course for the fall semester."

"I . . . er, yes, I have, but . . ." Her voice faded under the intense blaze of blue from his eyes.

"But . . . ?" Paul prompted.

Confused, shaken, Andrea said the first thing to pop

into her rattled mind. "I'm no longer certain. I might go back east . . . back home."

"Andrea!" Celia exclaimed from the doorway. "What are you saying?" Carrying the wine bottle in one hand and an ice bucket in the other, she crossed the patio to her niece. "You didn't mention a word to me about changing your plans." Her usually bright hazel eyes were clouded by concern.

"I thought everything was settled," Blaine said, setting a large tray containing four delicate long-stemmed glasses and several wooden snack bowls on the deck table before relieving Celia of the ice bucket and bottle. "I believed you had decided to stay here with Celia while you completed your postgraduate work at Parker."

Carefully avoiding looking at the disturbing cause of her sudden confusion, Andrea glanced helplessly from Celia to Blaine. "I . . . I don't know." Andrea was floundering badly, and she knew it. Turning to face her aunt, she pressed back against the rail; the smooth wood dug into her spine.

Celia peered at her through the romantic but inadequate glow provided by the decorative patio lights. "Andrea, are you feeling strange again?"

"Strange?" Blaine repeated, frowning.

"Strange?" Paul echoed, sounding interested.

Andrea cringed inwardly. "Strange" aptly described her odd behavior. If she wasn't careful, she advised herself, they might all decide she was one crumbling cracker.

"She wasn't feeling well earlier today," Celia explained. She looked at Andrea, touching her heart with the gentleness of her smile. "I thought you were feeling better, sugar."

Taking control of her battered emotions, Andrea injected confidence into her voice. "I am." She moved her shoulders in a helpless shrug. "Maybe I'm feeling a little homesick. I'm sorry I upset you."

"You're missing your friends?" Celia asked astutely.

"Yes." In that instant, Andrea realized that it was true; she was missing her friends, her sisters of the soul. Suddenly she ached for one of the into-the-morning exchanges of ideas and confidences she'd shared with Alycia and Karla, even if she couldn't tell them about her dream lover. "Yes," she repeated softly. "I am missing my friends."

"You could visit them," Celia suggested, her eyes wistful, as if she had already lost her niece.

"Of course," Blaine agreed, correctly reading Celia's expression. "Classes don't start for over a week. You could fly east, visit with your friends for a week, and still be back in time for your first class."

Andrea was shaking her head before he'd finished speaking. "No, I can't. They're not there. Alycia's with Sean on a lecture tour, and Karla's hard at work setting up her art gallery in Sedona, Arizona."

Celia looked anxious. "Then you'll stay as planned?"

Tears of shame for upsetting Celia burned Andrea's eyes. "Yes," she said huskily, "I'll stay."

"I promise you won't regret your decision."

Startled by the guarantee Paul offered, Andrea forced herself to look at him. The patio lights reflected the sheen of amusement in his dark blue eyes. Her heartbeat increasing at an alarming rate, she pressed her spine painfully against the wooden rail and infused a note of teasing into her voice. "How do you know you can deliver on your promise?"

"I teach a wild earth studies course."

Andrea stared at him for a moment, then burst into laughter. "I can't wait," she said, realizing at that second that it was true. Another realization struck her in the very next second. If she let herself, Andrea knew she could like this man.

The tension humming on the air dissolved in the liquid sound of Andrea's laughter.

"Well, shall we drink this wine before it gets warm?" Blaine asked, his relief almost palpable. Not waiting for a response, he filled the four glasses and parceled them out. When each of them held a glass, he raised his. "Now, what should we drink to?" His rugged face took on a quizzical expression.

"The weather?" Celia asked ingenuously.

Blaine favored her with a wry look.

Paul grinned.

"The new fall fashions?" Andrea inquired with elaborate innocence, joining the fun.

Blaine snorted.

Paul laughed out loud.

"Aw, come on, guys," Blaine groused. "You can do better than that."

"Guys?" Celia widened her eyes.

"Guys?" Andrea fluttered her long eyelashes.

"Hardly," Paul drawled. "But I'll give you a toast." He held his glass aloft. "To the president"—he tilted his glass at Blaine—"the faculty"—he tipped the glass toward himself—"and the students at Parker"—he moved the glass once more to indicate Andrea—"and to an interesting and productive fall semester." Raising the glass, he took a long swallow of the sparkling gold liquid.

With murmurs of appreciation and agreement, Andrea, Celia, and Blaine followed suit. The ice now completely melted, they made themselves comfortable on the padded lounge chairs grouped around the deck table.

Curling into a chair, Andrea sipped her wine and nibbled on the cheese-flavored crackers from one of the snack bowls. She heard but registered little of the animated conversation between her companions. She was much too distracted by the tall man reclining lazily in the chair opposite her own.

Despite the ambiguity of her feelings and the shock she experienced every time she looked at him, Andrea had to admit that Paul Hellka fascinated her. Even with her inattention to the varied discussions, it soon became evident to her that he was erudite and amusing.

In fact, Paul, the physical man, was every bit as similar in character to Andrea's fantasy lover as he was in appearance. The similarities both unnerved and enthralled her.

At one point during a conversation concerning computers and software—a subject about which Andrea knew absolutely nothing, but Paul apparently knew a great deal—he moved his hand in a gesture so achingly familiar to Andrea she had to bite her lip to keep from gasping aloud.

He habitually moved his hand in precisely the same way when making a point.

He embodied perfection of appearance.

He was erudite and amusing.

But *he* was a figment of her imagination.

Paul Hellka was flesh and blood, real, a physical entity.

Logically, Andrea knew that meeting a real man who resembled a dream man was unlikely, and that meeting a real man who was an exact replica of a dream man was impossible.

And yet, incredible as it seemed, Andrea found herself seated directly opposite a living, breathing impossibility.

It was enough to blow a fuse in any rational person's mind, Andrea decided, sipping the last of her wine. Before she could set her glass on the table, Paul sprang from his chair with the supple grace of a cat. Plucking the bottle from the ice bucket, he tilted it over her glass.

"More?" He arched perfect black eyebrows.

Startled, Andrea glanced up and felt her gaze become entangled in a soft web of velvet blue. "Ah . . . yes, thank you." In breathless amazement, she watched him fill her glass without spilling a drop or shifting his eyes as much as a flicker from hers.

"You're welcome." His voice was as soft and as velvety dark as his eyes.

Andrea's breath eased from her lips when he released her gaze to return to his chair. She felt touched in an odd way, as if his piercing gaze had looked through the windows of her eyes into her mind and her heart and her soul. Shaken by the weird sensation, she rested her head against the cushioned chair back and closed her eyes.

Was she losing touch with reality?

Andrea stirred uneasily as she contemplated the thought that swam into her mind.

But which reality? she wondered. The reality of a full year of nightly dreams of a fantasy lover? Or the waking reality of the man seated near her?

Her fantasy man, her love, was very real to her, so real that she had still felt the quaking aftermath of their lovemaking inside her body after waking from her dream.

But Paul Hellka was real, too, Andrea reasoned. Paul

was a friend of Blaine's and Celia's. She could not have imagined him.

But her nocturnal lover was imaginary, Andrea acknowledged. She had created him out of her own idea of male perfection. Yet Paul was the living image of her nocturnal lover.

It would all make sense, Andrea mused, if she had met Paul before her first meeting with her dream man. A lot of people dreamed about other real people. But she hadn't met Paul, had never even seen him before today. And so it didn't make any kind of sense to Andrea.

Giving up the fruitless exercise of trying to make sense out of no-sense, Andrea tuned out of her own circular thoughts and into her companions' conversation.

Celia was telling the men about Andrea's reaction to her first sight of sharks.

"... We could see them clearly from the beach." Celia gave a backward wave of her hand to indicate the crescent beach at the base of the cliffs below the house. "I could actually see the shudder that ran through Andrea's body."

Three pairs of compassion-filled eyes turned to gaze at Andrea. She smiled and shrugged.

"You're afraid of sharks?" Paul asked.

"Umm." Andrea nodded. "Just the sight of those fins slicing through the water give me the creeps." She shivered. "I haven't so much as wet my feet in the ocean since."

Celia laughed. "It's true. She refuses to go in even when Blaine's down at the beach with us."

"Needless to say, my masculine ego is in shreds," Blaine drawled.

"Which is preferable to having your body in shreds," Andrea retorted.

"Oh, sugar," Celia murmured, "you've always loved the ocean, and as long as you're careful, it's perfectly safe to go into the water."

His movements as fluid as the tides, Paul turned his attention from Celia to Andrea. "If you'd like, I'll stop by one afternoon to take you swimming," he said. "I assure you, you have nothing to fear from the sharks."

A memory bell rang inside Andrea's head, but before she could follow the ringing to its source it was muffled by the melodic sound of her aunt's laughter.

"I don't know how you could resist accepting, sugar," Celia laughed. "That has got to be the most original approach I've ever heard."

Appearing unperturbed by Celia's teasing, Paul smiled and raised a questioning eyebrow at Andrea.

"I don't know. . ." Andrea's voice faded on a note of uncertainty that arose from something more intimate than her fear of sharks.

"Your aunt's right, Andrea," Blaine drawled, shooting a speculative glance at his friend. "You must admit that the professor's approach is original. It's also a singular honor . . . and in a state that's famous for beautiful women."

Singular honor? Beautiful women? Andrea frowned. Was Blaine implying that Paul was, if not actually celibate, very, very selective? she pondered, shifting her narrow-eyed, skeptical glance from Blaine to Paul.

Blaine nodded and grinned.

Paul continued to look unperturbed, highly amused, and curious about how she'd respond.

Andrea was certain she could say "Thank you, but no, thank you" and the subject would be dropped—at least by Celia and Blaine; they knew, had witnessed, how adroitly she evaded any and all male advances. But she wasn't certain of anything as far as Paul Hellka was concerned.

But Andrea was intrigued by the man. How, she asked herself, could she be other than intrigued? She had made the most electrifying, satisfying love with his imaginary double that very afternoon!

What to do?

Andrea endured the gentle regard in the depths of his blue eyes while she mentally teetered on the brink of decision. She saw his eyes flicker an instant before Paul issued a challenge that tipped the scales in his favor.

"Why are you afraid?" His voice was soft, tender, but contained a thread of provocation. "An afternoon at the beach, Andrea. Within sight of the house." His smile taunted. "I promise I won't lure you in over your head."

Andrea decided that his assurance was a many-faceted statement if she'd ever heard one. There were more meanings than words to his promise. Nevertheless, more intrigued than before, she also decided to accept his invitation.

"All right," she agreed. "Pick an afternoon." Though Andrea felt pressured, she was not beyond a touch of wry insouciance. "But I warn you, if I see as much as a shadow of a dark fin anywhere between the shoreline and the horizon, I am outta there."

"Fair enough," Paul replied. "Are you free tomorrow afternoon?"

Telling herself that she was imagining the clicking sound of a trap springing shut, Andrea slanted a helpless look at her aunt. "Well, I did promise Aunt Celia I'd take it easy for the next few days," she said, making an attempt to buy a little clear-thinking time.

Celia gave her a dry look and a chiding smile. "I'm positive an afternoon on the beach would be more beneficial than detrimental." She waved a hand. "Go and enjoy yourself."

"Yes, go," Blaine urged. "And to keep your aunt from being bored, I'll take her to lunch in San Francisco." He grinned. "I'll even allow her to drag me through those quaint little art galleries she loves."

Andrea was well and truly trapped and she knew it. There was no way Celia would agree to go off to San Francisco for the day knowing Andrea was rattling around the house alone. Thinking that, if she had to give in, she might as well do it gracefully, she bestowed her most charming smile on Paul.

"Tomorrow afternoon will be fine," she finally answered. "Will two o'clock be all right?"

Paul's smile was slow in forming and devastating in effect. "Since Celia will be out for lunch, suppose I arrange a picnic lunch for us?" Though he posed the question, he didn't wait for her to respond. "Shall we say twelve?"

Andrea sighed in surrender. "Twelve will be fine."

Worrying over her acceptance of Paul Hellka's invitation, Andrea lay awake and restless for long hours after the men had gone and the house was quiet.

Was she being schoolgirlish and overcautious? she asked herself. Besides being unbelievably handsome, Paul appeared to be a genuinely nice person. And yet, Andrea was fearful of becoming involved with him.

She knew why, of course; the resemblance between

Paul and her fantasy man was so uncanny it was nerve-racking.

Her fantasy man.

Her love.

It was the thought of her love and her dream memories of him that eventually lulled Andrea to sleep. Maybe *he* would tell her what to do, how to handle this man who walked in the physical world wearing *his* face.

Andrea was running through the mist. Tears streamed down her face. She couldn't find the path! She couldn't find him! She called to him again and again.

My love! My love! Where are you?

Her voice had no sound, no substance!

Still she ran on, stumbling, falling, struggling to her feet again, running, running. She had to find the path. The path would lead her to him.

The mist thickened and closed in around Andrea. She couldn't breathe; she couldn't see!

She was sobbing; a silent weeping she couldn't hear, but could feel like repeated knife thrusts in her soul. An inner, soundless cry filled her being.

Where are you? Where are you?

I love you!

Then, swirling slowly, the mist began to disperse. In the distance, Andrea could see the vague outline of the path. A great wave of relief washed over her. Then, as the narrow path became clearly visible, the wave receded.

He wasn't there.

He wasn't there!

And then, suddenly, he was there, separate yet seemingly a part of the mist. His form was hazy, shadowy, as insubstantial as her voice.

Filled with incredible joy, Andrea made to run to him, but she couldn't progress. Her legs moved, but she didn't get anywhere. With a silent cry, she called to him to help her, to come to her.

He didn't answer. He waved. Then he began to fade, blending into the mist.

Panic clutched at Andrea's heart. He was waving farewell! Her love was leaving her!

And then he was gone.

Overwhelmed by wild, rending grief, Andrea threw back her head and screamed in despair.

"My love, you promised me always! Don't leave me!"

Andrea woke with a start. Tears streamed down her face. Morning sunshine sparkled on the pristine air beyond her bedroom windows.

She was alone.

Chapter Four

THE DREAM MIST STILL clinging to her mind, Andrea felt weighted by foreboding and despair.

He was gone.

Silent sobs shook her trembling body. Her grief-stricken mind whirled with one question: Why had he left her?

The question expanded to fill her head: *Why had he left her?*

The mournful cry of the seabirds beyond her open window penetrated the fog clouding Andrea's mind. A shuddering sigh whispered through her lips as the last tendrils of dream mist dissolved. The racking sobs subsided; her tears slowed to a trickle.

It was only a dream, she comforted herself, clasping her arms around her shivering body.

Only a dream.

Andrea bit her lip; her aunt had said those very same

comforting words to her . . . was it only yesterday?

Only a dream.

A chill snaked up Andrea's spine. He had come to her nightly in her dreams for nearly a year. They had talked together, been quiet together, and, finally, made exquisite love together . . .

Was it only yesterday?

And now, with a tender smile and a wave of farewell, her fantasy lover was gone.

Dragging her depleted body from the bed, Andrea walked to the window to stare sightlessly at the shimmering ocean. The morning air was cool and sweet. It bathed her face and dried the last of her tears.

From her window Andrea could see the small crescent beach at the base of the low cliff below the house. A tiny sandpiper ran around in frantic circles in search of breakfast. A faint smile curved her lips as she watched the bird dodge the wavelets lapping the shore. The sand was golden in the morning sunlight. The water looked refreshing, inviting . . .

Andrea's thoughts splintered. The beach. The water. She had a date to spend the day on the beach, in the water. She had a date to spend the day with a man who was the living image of her fantasy man.

The living image.

Andrea became still as speculation exploded inside her mind.

Paul was the *living* image of her fantasy man!

Was it possible? Andrea shook her head. The idea forming in her mind was too bizarre to be contemplated. And yet, she mused, could it be possible . . . ? Now that she had met his image in Paul, had her fantasy lover stepped out of her dreams, believing her to be secure from loneliness in the company of his breathing reflection?

Ridiculous! Andrea chided herself. Her fantasy man was only a figment of her imagination! A lovely dream, but a dream nonetheless. And dreams, no matter how seductive, could not spill over into reality.

But hadn't she allowed her reality to spill over into her dreams? An inner voice whispered the mocking query.

Andrea went cold at the thought, slowly shaking her head in silent denial. It wasn't true! she assured herself. She wasn't a child. She knew the difference between waking reality and sleeping fantasy.

Oh, really? The inner voice taunted. Then why all this anguish? Why this agony? Why the angst? Wake up and smell the coffee, Andrea, before you find yourself lost to reality in a dream world of your own devising.

Like most reasonably normal adults, Andrea didn't appreciate being pressured . . . not even by her own inner protective mechanisms. Her immediate reaction was defensive.

Tossing her head defiantly—exactly the way her dream self had done the previous afternoon—Andrea turned away from the window and strode to the bed. In a flurry of furious activity, she moved around the bed, grumbling to herself as she pulled, tugged, and smoothed the sheets and covers into order.

She was an intelligent, well-educated young woman, Andrea raved silently, applying more energy than domesticity to the task of bed-making. And she was certainly not about to lose herself to a dream or to any other imaginary reality!

But what about your fervent declaration of love during yesterday's dream? The chiding inner voice continued to taunt her.

But it was only a dream, Andrea justified herself mutely. It wasn't real.

Right. It wasn't real. The inner voice took on a victorious purr. It was only a dream.

Andrea's hands stilled on the pillow she was plumping; the flower-strewn pillowcase was damp from her tears.

Only a dream.

The sigh that ruffled the quiet in the room was wrenched from Andrea's soul.

But it was such a beautiful dream. And now it was gone. He was gone.

Andrea had never in her life felt so forsaken and alone, not even after her father's death or her mother's defection or Zach's betrayal.

Hugging the pillow to her chest, she sank onto the bed. Deep inside, Andrea felt intuitively that her fantasy lover would never again come to her in her dreams. An emptiness of spirit yawned inside her body and her soul.

Andrea knew that her aunt Celia would always be there for her, and she felt that, at least to a certain extent, Blaine would be there, too, in much the same way Alycia and Karla had. But she also knew that basically she was on her own.

Intellectually Andrea knew she couldn't make it on her own by clinging to the memory of a dream lover. The memory was sweet . . . but it was just a memory nonetheless. Though she believed that dreams were closely related to reality, she knew they had no real substance. And she had to live and interact in the corporeal world . . . or step over the fine line between reality and fantasy.

On a sun-splashed late August morning, Andrea examined her mind, her heart, her soul, and her options.
Then, squaring her shoulders without conscious
thought, she chose to step back from the line and live to
the best of her considerable ability in the here and now
of physical reality.

The decision made, Andrea acted upon it. Jumping
up, she replaced the pillow on the bed and smoothed the
coverlet over it before dashing for the bathroom.

Her first order of business in the world of physical
reality was to eat breakfast with her aunt.

By the time Andrea strolled into the kitchen and
wished her aunt a cheery good morning, she had succeeded in burying the memory of her dream-time love
like precious treasure in the deepest recesses of her heart
and mind. Like shining jewels of hope, the memories
would always be there, just below the surface of the
everyday, if she should ever need them.

"Well, good morning!" Celia exclaimed. She briefly
examined Andrea's expression, then smiled with relief.
"I don't have to ask how you slept . . . You look rested
and terrific."

Andrea flashed her aunt a grin as she slid onto a
chair. "I do feel pretty good," she said, not commenting
on the quality of her slumber. Surprisingly, the moment
the assertion was out, she realized she really was feeling
pretty good. She reached across the table for the glass
pitcher of chilled orange juice. Her nostrils flared as she
caught the mouth-watering aroma wafting from a covered bread basket sitting next to the pitcher. As she
drew her arm back, pitcher in hand, Andrea raised her
brows in question. "Muffins?" she asked hopefully.

"Yes." Chuckling, Celia moved the basket closer to
Andrea. Her chuckle turned into full-throated laughter

when Andrea's nostrils twitched. "Strawberry, your favorite."

Andrea groaned, and snaked her hand beneath the steam-warmed napkin. After slathering butter on the muffin, she took a bite and murmured her appreciation of the fruity flavor. "Mmm, delicious." She swallowed the morsel, then frowned at Celia. "Why did you make so many?" She indicated the muffin-mounded container. "Are you expecting Blaine for breakfast?"

"No." Celia shook her head. "He said he'd be here at eleven." Her soft mouth curved into a knowing smile. "But I wouldn't be surprised if he decides to have a muffin and a cup of coffee before we leave for San Francisco." Picking up the ceramic coffee server, she poured the aromatic brew into Andrea's cup, then refilled her own before continuing, "Actually, I made a double batch of the muffins, in case you wanted to add some to your picnic lunch."

Reminded of her date with Paul, Andrea momentarily forgot to chew the bit of muffin she'd popped into her mouth. For an instant sheer panic clutched at her throat.

It had been several years since Andrea had spent more than a few moments with a man. Wary and distrustful, determined never again to give a man the opportunity to hurt her, she had adroitly avoided being with any man.

Steam curled from her cup to tickle her taste buds with the fragrant scent of Colombian coffee, stirring the memory of her own taunting inner voice less than an hour ago.

Yes, Andrea mused, absently chewing the muffin. Perhaps it was time she shoved the past behind her, where it belonged, and faced the present, including both male and female members of it. Maybe it was time to wake up and smell the coffee before it and her youth were burnt.

"Paul Hellka," she said, tilting her head to gaze at her aunt. "It's an unusual name." She arched her eyebrows. "Is it Greek?"

Celia's expression went blank. "You know, I'm not sure." She gave a light shrug. "I guess I just assumed it was. But I never really asked."

Andrea polished off her muffin and reached for her cup. "Have you known him long?" she asked, blowing on the steam before sipping the hot coffee.

"Hmm," Celia murmured, frowning. "About a year, I suppose." She was quiet a moment, then said, "Come to think of it, it's almost exactly a year. Blaine introduced me to him when he arrived here last summer to join the faculty at Parker. And that was near the end of August, a week or so before the start of the fall semester."

Not wanting to appear excessively curious, Andrea drank her juice and half of her coffee before venturing another unconcerned-sounding question.

"You said when he arrived here," she said in the most casual tone she could manage. "Arrived from where?"

"Texas," Celia replied at once.

"Texas?" Andrea was more than surprised, she was stunned. "Texas!" she repeated in an incredulous tone. In her opinion, Paul Hellka did not look anything like a westerner. But come to that, she thought, he didn't look like an easterner, either. "What was he doing in Texas?"

Celia laughed, and the sound of her laughter seemed to indicate that she shared Andrea's opinion. "Believe it or not, he was born there," she said, still laughing softly.

"Odd," Andrea murmured, the idea persisting that he really didn't seem to be a product of any particular section of the country.

Celia arched her eyebrows in surprise. "Odd? I'm not sure I understand what you mean."

"Oh, I don't know." Andrea shrugged. "I suppose he just doesn't look like my preconceived notion of a native Texan"—her smile was self-derisive—"which, I admit, was fostered by Hollywood stereotypes."

"You mean, like all criminals should have scars?" Celia's smile was both wry and dry. "Or all the good guys must wear white hats?"

"Exactly!" Andrea grinned.

"You know better," Celia chided, her lips twitching from the need to return her niece's grin. "But you do have a point."

Andrea composed her expression, but an impish light danced in the depths of her eyes. "Are you referring to the one at the top of my head?"

Celia lost the battle against her twitching lips. "No, you teasing brat," she said lovingly. "I mean that Paul looks more European than western. And understandably so, since his parents were immigrants who settled in the American West, somewhere in the Big Bend area." Her tiny frown was contemplative. "If I remember correctly, both of Paul's parents are scientists."

"How did he ever wind up here, in California?" Andrea asked, while inwardly denying an unusual interest in the man.

"Economics," Celia answered, then smiled at the expression of confusion that washed over Andrea's face. "As Blaine explained it to me, he literally bought Paul away from the small Texas college where he was teaching at the time."

Andrea asked the question that immediately sprang into her mind. "Why? I mean, I was under the impression that professors were a dime a dozen these days. Why did Blaine buy this one particular educator?"

"Because he's brilliant," Celia said simply. "According to Blaine, who *does* know his business, Paul's credentials are not only impressive but damn near awesome."

This information coincided with the bits and pieces Andrea had garnered from her small cadre of new friends, all of whom were, at one level or another, students at Parker. According to them, the earth studies professor was "totally max"—the best in the business. And, although Andrea had completed an earth studies course in her freshman year of college, preparatory to her aerospace studies, her new friends' vocal admiration of Paul Hellka had inspired her to include his class in her graduate studies.

It seemed strange to Andrea now that she had never heard his name mentioned during any of the rap sessions she'd sat in on with her friends throughout the summer. Until Melly had enlightened her yesterday, every member of the small group had simply referred to him as "the prof," and that in tones of unabashed hero worship.

As if mentioning his name had somehow magically conjured him out of the air, Blaine rang the doorbell a second or two after Celia finished speaking.

"Oh, Lord!" Celia exclaimed. "It can't be eleven already!" She glanced at the kitchen clock, then shot out of her chair. She called instructions to Andrea as she dashed from the room. "Sugar, will you let Blaine in and keep him company while I get my act together?" Since she obviously knew what Andrea's response would be, she didn't wait to hear it. "Give him a cup of coffee and a muffin," she went on. "That'll keep him happy for a few minutes."

Already heading for the door, Andrea smiled as her aunt's musical voice wafted through the house to her.

"Good morning, gorgeous." Blaine greeted Andrea with a broad grin and a kiss on her cheek. "Don't tell me, let me guess," he drawled as he stepped into the house. "Our beautiful Celia just this minute ran into her bedroom to finish dressing." He raised his dark brows. "Right?"

"As rain," Andrea concurred, shutting the door. She grimaced as she turned to face him. "Whatever that means."

"It means I'm right," Blaine said, his grin growing. "Okay, what did our sweet lady tell you to do to keep me company?" he asked dryly, revealing how very well he knew and understood Celia Trask.

"Give you a cup of coffee and a strawberry muffin," Andrea replied, swinging away and heading back to the kitchen, confident he'd be right on her heels.

"That woman knows me much too well," Blaine observed in a rueful but amused tone, falling into step with Andrea.

Andrea tidied the kitchen while Blaine devoured two muffins and drank two cups of coffee. The room was spotless, and Blaine replete, before Celia breezed into the kitchen. Dressed in pale green slacks, high-heeled strappy sandals, and a white over-blouse splashed with flowers in mauve and rose, she presented a picture of casual elegance.

Blaine's eyes glazed over at first sight of Celia.

Standing by the sink, feeling like a fifth wheel, Andrea felt a twinge of envy. Blaine's love for Celia blazed, unconcealed and unchecked, from his dark eyes.

A yearning ache filled Andrea's being, and though she was genuinely happy that her aunt had at last found a love she could openly declare, Andrea couldn't help wondering how it felt to love and be loved that devotedly.

The ache lasted but an instant. A bubble of laughter rose to smother it. Her laughter erupted as Blaine whisked Celia out of the house . . . while she was in the middle of giving her niece last-minute instructions.

"I've left dinner in the fridge, Andrea," Celia called over her shoulder.

"Don't look for us until you see us, gorgeous," Blaine shouted, shutting Celia's door and then his own with solid-sounding thuds.

Andrea was still smiling as she returned to the kitchen. Her smile vanished when she glanced at the clock. Paul would be arriving in less than half an hour! With a soft yelp, she dashed out of the room.

She was frowning into the full-length mirror on the back of her bathroom door when the sound of the doorbell peeled through the house.

Paul!

Andrea's throat went dry as his name sprang into her mind. Her teeth caught her bottom lip as her eyes flashed to the door, then back to her reflection.

Suddenly the French-cut one-piece swimsuit she'd worn confidently all summer seemed much too skimpy. Her nervous fingers tugged at the edges of the material where the suit arched over her hipbones, revealing the long expanse of her slender, shapely legs.

Andrea groaned.

The doorbell pealed again.

In desperation, Andrea pulled on a cover-up and tied it snugly around her slim waist. She raised her eyes and groaned again. The terry-cloth robe barely covered her thighs.

Once again the doorbell pealed.

Andrea sighed. The robe would have to do. Making a face at herself in the mirror, she rushed from her bedroom to the front door. She was panting when she reached the door . . . but at least she was breathing. Becoming entangled with the sudden increase of her heartbeat, her breathing ceased altogether when she pulled the door open.

Looking too handsome to be real, Paul was leaning against the door frame, his body relaxed, his expression patient. His attire consisted of a loose stark-white shirt, which brushed the tops of his thighs. Andrea assumed the garment concealed his swim trunks. His long, smooth legs were exposed. His narrow feet were barely covered by leather sandals.

"Hi." His voice was low and attractive; his smile was slow and devastating. "Ready to face the beach?"

She could face anything with him.

The startling thought jolted Andrea, but she was breathing again . . . too rapidly, but breathing.

"Hi," she responded in a throaty voice she hardly recognized as her own. "Yes, I'm ready. I just have to get my things. Would you like to come in?"

"No." Paul shook his head briefly. Sunlight glinted blue sparks off the ruffled strands of his black hair. "I'll walk around and meet you at the patio steps." His eyes delved into the hazel depths of hers.

"Ah . . . fine." Andrea felt the effects of his stare to the very depths of her soul. "I . . . I'll meet you there."

He pushed away from the door frame.

She backed away from the doorway.

"Go," he whispered, releasing his visual hold.

Freed from the bond of his eyes, and confused by the crazy quilt of sensations leaping pell-mell along her nervous system, Andrea swung the door shut as she spun away at a run to collect her beach bag and the muffins she'd transferred to a plastic storage bag.

The descent to the beach wasn't arduous, just a bit tricky. With a blanket slung around his neck, and toting a cooler chest, Paul assisted Andrea over the rough spots with his free hand, leaving her skin tingling with awareness of him.

The day was perfect. A cloudless blue sky arched overhead. Sunlight, like gold coins, skimmed across the deeper blue of the ocean. A gentle breeze wafted mistily off the water, robbing the sun's rays of their burning sting. Seabirds squabbled and swooped to pluck tidbits from the shore.

The zephyr played with Andrea's hair, swirling the shoulder-length strands around her face. Too aware of Paul, and hiding it by staring out over the water, she absently raised her hands to anchor the mass to her head.

"Don't."

Andrea stiffened when his long fingers encircled her wrists to pull her hands away.

"Leave it free," Paul said softly, close to her ear. "Let it fly."

"It gets in my mouth," Andrea said in a hoarse, barely discernible voice.

"Lucky hair."

His voice was so low Andrea wasn't sure she heard him correctly. "Wh-what?" she asked shakily.

"Nothing." He was standing so close she could feel

his breath whisper over the back of her neck. "Stand still, I'll fix it for you."

He released his loose grip on her wrists. Andrea felt him move or bend, and then he brought his hands back to her head. Her scalp tingled as he raked his fingers through her hair, and she shivered when they brushed the nape of her neck. A sigh of protest lodged in her throat when he dropped his hands and stepped back.

"There, that should hold it."

Curious, Andrea raised her hands to the back of her head. Her eyes widened as she examined his handiwork with her fingers. He had neatly braided her hair! She couldn't feel as much as one errant wisp. And he had secured it . . . how? Frowning, Andrea turned to stare at him.

A tender smile curved his lips. "There's a question?" he asked quietly.

"How did you do that?" Andrea demanded.

"The braiding?" he teased.

Andrea shook her head. "How did you fasten it?"

He stooped, and when he rose he was holding a curled string of dried seaweed between his thumb and forefinger. "Everything we require can be found somewhere in nature, Andrea," he said, swinging the plant stem gently.

He had bound her hair with a dried weed! Indignant, Andrea glared at him. "A weed?" she yelped.

Paul smiled at her, revealing hard teeth that glistened a glaring white in contrast to his burnished skin. "That weed is harmless and as much a part of nature as you are."

Andrea's indignation melted in the warmth of his smile. "Well, if you say so," she muttered, offering him a tentative smile tinged with teasing. "Just so you never ask me to eat any of that gloppy wet stuff."

Paul tilted his head back and roared with laughter. "Gloppy wet stuff?" he repeated when he could finally speak. "Don't you know that kelp is one source of iodine?"

Andrea looked unimpressed. "I'll take mine in salt, thank you."

"Oh, I can see I'm in for a very interesting semester with you in my class," Paul said, laughing as he turned to spread the blanket out on the sand.

"Scared, Professor?" Andrea taunted, not even aware that she had lost her nervousness about being alone with him.

"No." Paul slanted a grin at her. "I'm looking forward to it," he returned her taunt. "Aren't you?"

"Yes," Andrea admitted. "But right now I'm looking forward to whatever lunch you've brought." Her expression turned mock-fierce. "And it better not be seaweed."

The meal Paul provided was almost as perfect as the day. There was fruit salad to begin, crisp vegetables cut into bite-size pieces, a long loaf of crusty French bread, which they ate with chunks of a cheese Andrea didn't recognize but thoroughly enjoyed and of course there were the strawberry muffins. Between bites, they savored the delicate flavor of chilled California chenin blanc. While the food slowly disappeared, they talked of this and that—what she thought of California, the fast-approaching fall semester, her preference for white wine, his preference for strong cheese—inconsequential in sound, considerable in insight.

Without being aware of it, Andrea laughed often. But she did notice that each time she laughed, Paul's eyes seem to glow from within.

When they were finished, they worked together, swiftly, competently, not fumbling, never bumping, as if they intuitively knew their individual tasks, repacking the cooler and smoothing the blanket.

Replete—stuffed, actually—Andrea lay back on the blanket, surrendering her body to the sun. She felt Paul move and raised her arm to shade her eyes. He was standing beside the blanket, his arms stretched over his head, tendons and muscles rippling as he pulled off the white shirt. His body gleamed a burnished gold in the direct rays of the sun.

For an instant, Andrea forgot to breathe, her heart forgot to beat. He was the most breathtaking, heart-stopping thing she had ever had the privilege to gaze upon.

Strangely, in contrast to the shock of wavy black hair on his head and the silky forest of curls on his chest, the rest of Paul's body was hairless and smooth. His shoulders and chest were broad and yet, as Andrea had noticed the day before, were free of the pumped-up, bunched-muscled look. His waist and hips were narrow, his belly not merely flat but concave. His long arms and legs were perfectly formed.

His overall appearance had a riveting effect on Andrea, but what claimed her unwilling attention was the narrow scrap of white material that swathed his loins.

The sight made her blood run cold, then hot. She felt chilled, then flushed. He was little more than a stranger to her, and yet, it was as if her body knew him in the most intimate way possible.

Feeling shaken, confused, disoriented, her eyes seeing nothing, and everything, Andrea lay breathless and immobile, staring, staring.

"Andrea."

His low voice was a soft caress and a rude awakening. Flustered, embarrassed, Andrea flicked her eyes to his, and immediately shied away from the understanding she read in the soft blue depths. She turned her head away when he sank to his knees beside her.

"There is no shame in admiring the human form," he said, not touching her, but stroking her with his tender tone. "I've been admiring your body ever since . . . ever since we met."

Andrea heard and wondered at his brief pause, the slight break in the even tenor of his voice, but then the question in her mind was drowned by the flow of his voice washing over her senses.

"Your body is beautiful. Your skin is soft and silky," he whispered. "I feel no shame in admiring the gentle contour of your slender hips, the delicate curve of your breasts and the appealing cast of your lovely features." He lay on the blanket beside her. His voice was the only part of him that touched her. "And what shame should I feel in admiring that most feminine part of you, that exquisite mound of utter beauty and ultimate, infinite pleasure?"

"Stop!" Andrea cried in a raspy whisper. "Paul, please stop! I can't bear any more. I can't . . ."

It was too late. Though he had not touched her, Andrea's body had felt, and reacted, as if to a lover's caress, to every whispered word he'd spoken. Her mind was on fire; her body responded in the most natural of ways to the consuming conflagration.

Her sensibilities cringed in embarrassment.

Her body rejoiced in release.

Chapter Five

"I'M SORRY." PAUL'S SOFT voice revealed sorrow . . . but not regret.

They were lying side by side on the sun-warmed blanket, close but not touching.

"I'm not." The utter truth of her reply struck Andrea as she spoke. She still felt slightly embarrassed, but she was not sorry for the thrilling effect his words had had on her.

"I don't want you to feel that I set out deliberately to manipulate you," he murmured. "My only wish was to ease the embarrassment and shame you were suffering."

"I know." A faint smile curved Andrea's soft mouth. "I'm not a child, Paul. I do understand willing reception." Her smile slanted wryly at the analogy that sprang to her mind, then to her lips. "What I experienced was not unlike hypnosis, in that one absolutely cannot be put under if the conscious mind refuses to be submerged."

Gathering her courage, she turned her head to look at him.

"I like that." His soft tone was loud with approval.

Incredibly, to Andrea's surprise, she blushed with pleasure at his praise.

Paul laughed softly, but spoke seriously. "And you were not alone. I shared every one of those sweetly ecstatic moments with you, Andrea."

Andrea's thoughts splintered, then regrouped in fragments.

He didn't . . .

He couldn't have . . .

Could he . . . ?

Had he . . . ?

"No, Andrea." Paul stared deep into her eyes.

Andrea blinked. Had he read her mind? Alarm shivered through her. His eyes spoke to her with eloquent silence. No, of course he hadn't read her mind, she thought with relief. Reading her mind hadn't been necessary; her fractured thoughts had probably been written clearly across her face. When the cloud of uncertainty dispersed from her eyes, he continued speaking in the same soft, reassuring tone.

"The sensations I experienced were psychological, not physical, in nature. But my experience was no less intense than your own."

"I . . . I . . ." Andrea had to swallow against a tightness in her throat before she could go on. "Nothing like this has ever happened to me before."

"Then I feel doubly honored."

Andrea frowned. "Doubly?"

"Yes." Paul smiled. "Honored to have been the one responsible for your experience, and honored to have shared the beauty of that experience with you."

Tears misted Andrea's eyes. What manner of man was this Paul Hellka? she asked herself in wonder. She had never met any other man with the depth of understanding, compassion, and sensitive empathy this man possessed.

The moisture clinging to her lashes weighted her eyelids. Drained by the physical experience she'd been through and by the mental groping she'd muddled through, Andrea hardly noticed the downward pull of her lashes.

She sighed and relaxed. A lulling voice from beside her whispered into her slumberous state of mind.

"Sleep, Andrea. Rest. You have nothing to fear."

There was no mist. Brilliant sunshine bathed the earth with warmth and light.

Calm, serene, and happy, Andrea strolled along the familiar path. She was alone, and as she walked she hummed softly to herself.

As she approached the twisted tree in the clearing, a gentle smile of remembrance curved her lips. She paused a moment to glance at the grassy floor of the clearing beneath the tree. Then, without a backward glance, she continued on along the path.

The scent of the sea grew ever stronger as she neared a curve in the path. On sight of the bend, Andrea's heartbeat quickened, her pulse raced, her spirit soared.

She was almost there.

Increasing her step, she hurried along the gently curving path. The scent of the sea was now pervasive.

She was almost home!

Overhead a seabird swooped. As it came out of its dive, the bird sent forth a mournful cry.

* * *

Andrea's eyes flew open, then immediately narrowed to slits in defense against the glare of midday sunlight. Overhead to her left, a sea gull squawked its raucous cry.

Shaking the dream-webs from her mind, Andrea sat up and glanced at the expanse of blanket beside her. She was alone. Paul was gone.

Where was he? Andrea was startled by the anxiety that accompanied her question. Suddenly, inexplicably uneasy, she scrambled up off the blanket. The sun-baked sand burned the tender soles of her feet.

The uneasiness growing inside her, Andrea glanced around the small crescent-shaped beach. Natural rock jetties thrust into the ocean at either end of the beach, forming a small U-shaped cove, the left stroke of the U shorter than the right. It would have been impossible to miss seeing him if he'd been strolling along the shore.

Raising one hand to shade her eyes, Andrea gazed out over the restless water. Beyond the protective confines of the cove, the Pacific rushed toward the shore, slowly building waves that crashed against the rock jetties, spraying sun-sparkled water high into the air.

And out farther, beyond the curling waves, Andrea spotted the bobbing head of an intrepid swimmer.

Paul! His name erupted from her throat even as it sprang into her mind.

"Paul!" Andrea knew it was impossible for him to hear her, but still she called out again. "Paul!"

To her astonishment, he thrust one long arm into the air and waved. The action struck a familiar chord inside Andrea, but she ignored the odd sensation in her eagerness to call him in. Shouting, she raced toward the shoreline.

"Paul, come in! Please come in closer to shore!"

Again, to her amazement, he appeared to hear her. He gave another wave, then turned and began swimming for shore.

Closing her eyes, Andrea sighed with relief. Unwilling to examine the depth of her feelings, she opened her eyes to check his progress. The sight that met her horrified gaze made her blood run cold.

A short—too short—distance behind Paul, six arched black fins sliced through the water in silent menace. Stark terror clawed at Andrea's throat as she watched those fins close in on him.

Sharks!

Andrea opened her mouth to cry out.

Nothing.

Deadly fear snaked through Andrea's body, freezing her to the hot sand. In her mind's eye, she could see the large, gaping jaws and jagged curving teeth. Bile flooded her mouth. She worked her throat, swallowing, swallowing, forcing down the silencing obstruction of abject terror.

The gliding fins grew nearer to the swimming man, then began to circle him in ever diminishing cycles. Unable to move, breathe, think, Andrea watched in horrified fascination, expecting, dreading, the inevitable fury of thrashing water and the sickening spread of crimson on the undulating surface of sapphire blue.

No. No. The litany began inside her head, and grew until her skull could no longer contain it.

"No! Paul! No!"

Suddenly Andrea broke free of the paralyzing fear. Screaming his name, she ran toward the water.

"Andrea. No."

The breeze carried the sound of his voice to her. As if by command, her legs refused to move . . . The sensation was similar to the dream she'd had the day before, only this was no dream, it was a living nightmare.

Sobbing, gasping for breath, Andrea stood, seemingly rooted in the sand, crying, praying, sobbing his name. Then, suddenly, the sobs lodged in her throat and she stared, incredulity stunning her mind as she watched the sharks circle Paul and then glide back out to sea.

In numbed bewilderment, Andrea stood mute, staring at the man swimming at a leisurely pace toward shore, toward her. She was too shaken to call out to him to hurry. She was too traumatized to feel relief.

The shock freezing her mind and senses slowly began to recede with each long, smooth stroke that brought Paul closer to the calm waters inside the cove. Her pent-up breath began to ease from her constricted chest.

Too soon.

Andrea saw something from the corner of her eye. Afraid to look, yet knowing she must, she turned and skimmed a gaze over the roiling waves near the rocky right arm of the enclosure. Her insides liquefied.

The sharks were back. Coming in more swiftly, the dark fins seemed to slide through the turbulent waves building to fling themselves against the rocks. They were all around Paul before she could open her mouth to scream a warning.

Dear God! No!

The inner scream seemed to unlock the odd immobility anchoring her legs to the beach. Andrea didn't pause to consider that she could do nothing to help him, nothing except lose her life with him. Her horrified eyes riveted to the encircling fins, she began to run.

Andrea was waist deep in water when she came to a sudden halt. Her expression of stark terror gave way to wide-eyed wonder as she saw a long, glistening steel-gray body leap from the waves in an arching swoop, then dive again, long thin snout first.

Dolphins!

Never noticing the chill of the sixty-degree temperature of the water lapping her chest, unmindful of the tears streaming down her face to mingle with another salty moisture, Andrea laughed aloud as she watched the beautiful mammals swim and leap playfully around Paul. Like an echo of her own, she heard Paul's laughter ripple across the waves to her.

Then the dolphins, too, were gone, streaking away around the rocky jetty as swiftly as they'd appeared. Repressing an urge to wave good-bye to the sleek creatures, Andrea observed them until they disappeared. Then she returned her concerned attention to the man swimming toward her.

Hurry, please hurry, Andrea urged him silently, thinking his progress too languid, too slow. The frayed edges of fear still danced along her nerves. Fighting reactive tears, she pleaded mutely. Please, Paul, please hurry, hur—

Andrea shuddered; her mind rebelled in strident protest.

Not again!

The solitary evil-looking fin slid through the water, around the right-side jetty, and directly toward Paul.

This was not possible! Andrea's emotion-battered mind whimpered. It was too much . . . much too much.

Andrea's warning cry lacked strength. "Swim, Paul! There's another one behind you!" She saw him turn his head, and then he did the strangest thing imaginable.

Paul stopped swimming. Treading water, he slowly rotated his body in unison with the circling shark. The enormous fish closed the circle around Paul with each successive sweep. When the fin was within a few feet of him, Paul thrust his arm to one side. The fin disappeared beneath the surface of the ocean. When it again broke the surface, the fin was moving away, heading out to sea.

Andrea was stupefied. What in heaven's name had caused that monster to turn away? she wondered in senses-dulled amazement. Then a memory stirred at the fringes of her mind. Hadn't she once heard or read somewhere that a shark could be deflected by a hard rap on the snout? When he'd flung his arm to the side, had Paul delivered a . . . ?

Andrea's thoughts scattered. Paul had swum close enough to shore to stand. After slicking his hair back from his face, he walked toward her. He didn't look terrified or traumatized or even frightened. He was smiling!

His smile broke her.

Emitting a strangled half-sob, half-laugh, Andrea ran to him and launched her trembling body toward the solid strength of his. Clasping him tightly around the waist, she buried her face in the wet silk on his chest and wept.

Paul went still and rigid for a moment. Then Andrea felt his chest expand as he inhaled, heard the deep sigh he expelled an instant before his arms closed around her in a breathtaking confidence-restoring embrace.

He was safe . . . safe! The realization reduced Andrea to a quaking mass, capable of nothing more than a babble. "Paul . . . sharks . . . I was petrified . . . I wanted to help . . . The dolphins . . . I couldn't believe . . . I . . ."

"Andrea." His low voice was as soothing as the hand he stroked lightly down her spine.

Uncaring of the tears pooling in her eyes, Andrea lifted her head to gaze up at him. His sculpted features were softened by infinite tenderness. In contrast, a spark of raw sensuality smoldered in his dark eyes. He lowered his head, slowly, as if in defiance of his own will. His voice deepened to a rough-velvet groan.

"Oh, Andrea."

His lips touched Andrea's with the delicacy of sheer gossamer. His mouth made no demand on hers. His kiss was sweet, calming, reassuring.

Andrea sighed.

Paul made a sound, a murmur, a sigh; then he molded his mouth to the soft contours of hers. The pressure his mouth applied to hers was controlled and barely perceptible. The hands he slid over every inch of her back were warm and restless, a tactile denial of his passionless kiss.

Andrea felt the sweetness of his kiss, the hungry movement of his hands, to the outermost edges of her being. Her soul took flight. Her body melted. Her mind surrendered. Moaning softly deep in her throat, she parted her lips and pressed her mouth to his. And for one glorious instant, she caught a glimpse of paradise. The instant ended too soon and left a bone-deep yearning inside her with its passing.

"No, Andrea," Paul whispered, drawing his head back. "Not like this. You're too vulnerable now."

"You could have been killed!" she exclaimed, shuddering as the memory slammed back into her mind.

"No." Paul smiled and shook his head. "I was never in any danger." His smile curved into a teasing tilt. "I told you there was nothing to fear."

"Nothing to fear?" Andrea cried indignantly, pulling out of his embrace. "Those were sharks out there!" she said in an agitated gasp . . . as if he hadn't known.

"Dolphins," Paul corrected her, his lips twitching.

The ordeal had stretched Andrea's nerves to the limit, and they were beginning to unravel with reaction. "Paul, I know what I saw!" she said heatedly. "And I know there were sharks out there!"

Reaching out to her, Paul curled his hand loosely around her arm. "Come," he said gently. "You're upset. I'll take you back to the house."

The terror she had suffered, the relief of anticlimax, and even his gentleness—especially his gentleness— did Andrea in. Tearing her arm free, she stepped away and said in a measured tone, "I told you earlier that I am not a child, Paul. Don't treat me like one."

"Treat you like a child?" His smile hinted at a deep inner longing. "Ah . . . Andrea, if you only knew."

Reaction was taking its toll on her. Andrea turned it on him. "If I only knew what?" Once started, she couldn't stop. "I don't understand you. I don't understand what you're hinting at but not saying! I . . . I . . . Dammit! I'm going home!" Skirting around him, she ran up the beach. She was too angry and upset to recall that home was precisely where Paul had offered to take her.

He could have caught her without half trying.

It wasn't the first time Andrea had had the thought since running away from Paul hours ago.

In the intervening hours she had taken a shower, force-fed herself a piece of toast and a glass of milk, and cried a lot. The really infuriating thing was, Andrea didn't even know what she was crying about.

Calmer, but feeling restless and moody, Andrea curled up on a chaise longue to watch the sun do its spectacular nightly performance by vividly painting the sky with breathtaking hues as it slowly nose-dived into the horizon.

This evening, Andrea was supersensitive to the splashes of pink and red, gold and violet. A copper sheen gilded the deep blue of the sea. Nature was so glorious, she mused, sighing. Why did living have to be so painful at times?

One of those times had occurred when Paul had eventually made his way to the house from the beach. The very fact that he had lingered on the beach for over an hour after her precipitous flight hurt Andrea in a way she didn't—or wouldn't—understand. Reacting to the inner pain, she had displayed a cool, distant exterior.

Paul appeared neither dismayed nor deterred by her attitude. "You forgot your things," he said, smiling as he handed her the beach bag and the leftover muffins.

Refusing to be caught with her emotional guard down, Andrea dredged up a return smile and a civil tone. "Thank you for bringing them." She started to back away from the door. He stopped her without raising a hand, or his voice.

"Will you be all right?"

Andrea lifted her chin. "Of course," she said with assurance, lying through her teeth. She felt light-years away from all right. "I'm just a little tired," she went on, giving him the understatement of the century. "I shouldn't have fallen asleep in the sun . . . It . . . ah, always drains everything from me," she improvised—badly.

"I see."

Though his inflection didn't change, Andrea read the expression in his eyes and knew he saw through her. She knew that he knew that she was lying. Still, she continued in the same vein. "Yes, so I think I'll make it an early night." Grasping the door, she closed it partway as she stepped back. "Ah . . . I'll see you later." Her tone negated the promise in her words.

"Never doubt it," Paul murmured, reaching forward to tug the door from her trembling fingers. "You're enrolled in my class, remember?" Without waiting for an answer, he gently shut the door.

Andrea stared at the door for a full thirty seconds. Remember? Remember? she thought wildly. She only wished she could forget!

If anything, she had felt as if she were unraveling since he'd left her standing at the door, fighting tears born of confusion and frustration.

Still too tense to remain in one spot for more than a few minutes, Andrea jumped up and wandered through the house. After spending the last four years dodging her two flatmates, the house seemed too large, too empty.

As she was empty.

Shying away from the thought, Andrea went to her bedroom. The thought went with her. Empty. That was her story in a nutshell. Empty life. Empty dreams. Empty body. At the last thought, Andrea clapped her hand over her mouth to muffle a groan.

She had wanted him to fill the emptiness of her body.

With the silent acknowledgment, the memory of that afternoon came flooding into her mind, swamping Andrea all over again. She had told Paul she didn't understand . . . It was probably the biggest understatement of her life.

Weakened by trauma and reaction, Andrea was powerless against the questions that hammered inside her mind.

Why had she responded the way she had to his voice?

Why had he said there were no sharks?

Why had he put her away from him?

Why? Why? Why?

The questions pounded, pounded in her head. There were no answers, only more questions. Andrea grimaced and rubbed her forehead. She might not have any answers, but she was developing one beauty of a headache.

Andrea was rummaging in the medicine cabinet for some aspirin when her aunt returned home.

"Andrea, sugar, we're back," Celia called from the living room. "Are you decent?"

That depends on your definition of the word, Andrea replied silently, flushing with the memory of her experience on the beach. "Yes," she answered aloud.

"Then come have a glass of wine with us," Celia called. "I want to show you what I bought."

Despite the throbbing in her temples, Andrea had to smile. When it came to shopping, Celia was like an excited, wide-eyed child; every purchase delighted her. Since coming to stay with her aunt, Andrea had often found herself hoping that she could retain just a smidgen of Celia's enthusiasm for life when she herself reached her middle years.

"I'll be there in a minute," Andrea said, tossing two of the white tablets into her mouth. She grimaced with distaste as one of the tablets scraped her tongue on the way down.

Damn! Andrea thought as she walked into her bedroom. She didn't know which was worse, the pill or the pain. She scooped her lightweight robe off the bed as she passed by. Pulling the cover-up over her thigh-length nightshirt, she crossed the room to the door.

Andrea didn't really want a glass of wine. Her head-ache was doing fine without any help from the fruit of the vine. But she had hopes that the animated company of her aunt and Blaine might banish the tormenting questions that had caused the blasted headache in the first place.

In the end, Andrea had the glass of wine anyway and, to her surprise, the throbbing ache subsided some-what—whether from the wine or the lively conversa-tion, she didn't know, nor did she care. She was simply grateful that the pain had eased.

Celia proudly displayed her shopping loot to Andrea. Then taking turns, and sometimes both speaking at the same time, she and Blaine told Andrea about their day.

When Andrea finally retired for the night, she mused that, although Celia's and Blaine's day in San Francisco sounded like fun, it was rather ordinary in comparison to the hours she had spent with Paul.

All the memories, tension, and drama—along with the accelerated pounding in her head—rushed back with the thought of his name to haunt Andrea.

Thinking about taking more aspirin, she started for the bathroom, then stopped short, her eyes glittering with the light of firm determination.

Pills hadn't helped. Wine hadn't helped. A few pleasant hours of lighthearted conversation hadn't helped. Perhaps, Andrea reasoned, it was time she did something to help herself.

Without giving conscious thought to her movements, Andrea began to pace off the width of her bedroom.

All right, start from the beginning, she told herself. Let's see if we can make any sense at all out of the odd things that have happened since the advent of the flesh and blood man who is the mirror image of a fantasy man.

Her brow puckered in concentration, Andrea paced the soft carpet, back and forth, back and forth, trying to make sense of the seemingly senseless.

The first order of sense alignment was the acceptance of the fact of Paul Hellka's existence. It seemed impossible—had seemed impossible to Andrea from her first sight of him through the window of the coffee shop. But Paul was most assuredly real. He walked, he talked, he laughed, he . . . Andrea's breath caught, but she forced herself to complete the thought. He kissed. She moaned. Lord, did he kiss!

Okay, pull yourself together and get on with it, Andrea chided herself. Paul might look as if he'd walked out of a dream—her dream, but he was real. And, as if the fact that Paul so closely resembled her fantasy man weren't enough, the similarities didn't end there.

Andrea knew those similarities were the root of her headache and her restless pacing. With cool intent, she skimmed those similarities, one by one, from her memory.

In her dreams, her love had said, "You have nothing to fear. . ." In reality, Paul had repeatedly said, "You have nothing to fear. . ."

In her dreams, her love had tenderly opened the doors of paradise to her. In reality, Paul had tenderly given her a similar exquisite experience.

While she had been running around frantically in the mist of her dreams, her love had called to her . . . "Andrea." While she was running frantically toward the water that afternoon, Paul had called to her . . . "Andrea."

Her dream love had raised his arm in farewell. Paul

had raised his arm to her from the water in exactly the same way.

Were all those similarities happenstance? Mere coincidence? Andrea demanded of her tired mind, all the while pacing, pacing. And even if they were, she followed the thought thread warily, there was still something very strange about Paul Hellka.

Andrea shook her head impatiently. What was it about the man that threw her off balance? From their attitude, it was obvious that neither Celia nor Blaine considered Paul in any way strange or different.

But he *was* different! Andrea insisted silently, raking a trembling hand through her hair. He had tied off her braid with seaweed! Well, that wasn't too different, she conceded. But what about that incredible release she'd experienced? Paul had brought her to ecstasy without laying a hand on her!

But he had caressed the most sensitive erogenous zone in the human body, a tiny voice whispered from the depths of her consciousness.

Paul had caressed her mind.

Andrea came to a dead stop. Her throat worked against the tightness of fear. Her fingers flexed, in, out, curling and uncurling. Moisture dewed her brow as she strained to hear the murmur from the deepest part of her consciousness. When it came, the information sent a chill through her body.

Paul swam with the sharks.

Like a sleepwalker, Andrea slowly moved her head from side to side in repudiation. It wasn't possible for a human to swim with the sharks. Sharks were mindless scavengers. They were huge, mean eating machines! Once more the murmur worked its way to the surface of her consciousness.

Think. Remember.

Closing her eyes, Andrea cast her mind back to the scene, bringing the memory into vivid clarity. Terror crawled through her body as she relived the sight of those evil-looking fins slicing through the water. Joy overcame terror as she once again viewed the beauty of the dolphins at play. And horror returned with the image of a solitary fin closing in on Paul. If he hadn't thrust his arm out to strike—

No!

Andrea's eyes flew open. Staring, staring, she saw nothing of the room around her, and everything of that traumatic moment. She saw . . . saw—

Paul had not flung his arm to one side to strike the shark! He had reached out to stroke the monster!

Andrea blinked and glanced around fearfully. She was not on the beach, she was safe in her room. And still she felt a fearful trembling inside, a trembling caused by the question revolving inside her mind.

What manner of man was this?

Chapter Six

A LIGHT TAPPING LURED Andrea from the depths of slumber. Struggling against the enticement of forgetfulness, she stirred and opened her eyes when the tapping came again, this time followed by a soft call.

"Andrea, are you awake?" Celia's voice was raised slightly to penetrate the closed bedroom door. "Melly's on the phone. Should I ask her to call back later?"

Melly? Andrea blinked and stared at the ceiling. Full consciousness came in a sudden rush. "No, Aunt Celia," she replied. "I'll be there in a minute." She sat up and swung her legs over the side of the bed. Her body felt heavy; her mind felt dull. "What time is it?" she asked in a dry croak.

"It's eleven-twenty," Celia answered, her voice fading as she moved away from the door.

"Eleven-twenty!" Andrea exclaimed. She jumped up, then had to grab for the brass headboard to steady herself, as her head seemed determined to fly off her shoulders.

Andrew stood still until her whirling senses righted themselves; then she stumbled toward the door. The long night she had spent tossing and turning, along with the subsequent disjointed and confusing dreams she'd had after finally falling asleep, clung to the edges of her mind. Andrea was awake and moving, yet not fully with it.

Navigating from her room to the telephone mounted on the kitchen wall required every bit of concentration she could summon. Merely raising the receiver to her ear seemed like an enormous task.

"Hello." Andrea hardly recognized the cottony sound of her own voice. "Melly?"

"Are you all right?" Melly's usually bubbly voice was subdued by concern.

Will you be all right?

Andrea shivered at the memory echo of Paul's voice, and with a weak smile of gratitude accepted the small glass of fresh grapefruit juice Celia thrust into her hand. She took a long swallow to moisten her dry throat, and then a deep breath before replying to her friend. "I'm fine, Melly. I just woke up and I'm still a little groggy."

"Just woke up?" Melly sounded scandalized. "Andrea, it's nearly lunchtime!"

"Mmm . . ." Andrea glanced at the clock. Damned if it wasn't, she mused, yawning. "I know," she said aloud to her friend. "It was very late before I fell asleep, and I didn't sleep all that well. I guess that's why I overslept." Andrea frowned. Why was she making excuses to Melly? She certainly didn't owe her friend an explanation . . . Come to that, she didn't owe anybody an explanation!

"Oh, I see," Melly replied in a tone that said clearly that she didn't really see at all. Her tone was proof of her lack of insight as she continued in a chirpy voice, "I never have trouble falling asleep."

Lucky you. Andrea kept the thought to herself and said patiently, "Did you call for a specific reason or just to"—she fought back the word "babble" and inserted—"chat?" Andrea genuinely liked Melly; it was just that, sometimes, the younger woman's flightiness got to be a trifle too much.

"Oh! A reason, of course!" Melly exclaimed.

Beginning to feel as though she should be wearing a white jacket and plastic gloves, and wielding a tooth extractor, Andrea sighed. "Do you want to tell me the reason?" she asked patiently, eyeing the coffee carafe on the table with longing. "Or am I expected to guess?"

Melly gasped, then giggled—two endearing things Melly did quite often. "No, silly, of course you aren't expected to guess!" she again exclaimed—a third thing she did often.

And she calls *me* silly, Andrea thought wryly. "Then are you going to tell me what it is?" she prompted, her fuzzy mind losing the thread of the conversation.

Melly replied true to form. "What *what* is?"

Closing her eyes, Andrea leaned forward to rest her forehead on the smooth wall. "The reason you called, Melly," she answered with tired patience.

"Oh, yeah!" Melly giggled again. "Sara called me a few minutes ago to tell me that the gang's getting together this afternoon to have a last blast on the beach before fall classes begin," she finally explained. "Want to come?"

"The gang" consisted of a group of young people, ranging in ages from nineteen to thirty-one, who were all students attending Parker College. Andrea had more or less been absorbed into the group after becoming friends with Melly.

The beach. A shudder rippled through Andrea's body. She was on the point of declining the invitation when she suddenly reconsidered.

The beach where the gang usually held their parties was located several miles away from the little cove below her aunt's house. And though the cliffs rose from the edge of the sand, there were no enclosing rock jetties. It was not at all similar to the little crescent beach. And being with the usually high-spirited group might restore her *normal* sense of equilibrium.

"Did you fall asleep, Andrea?" Melly demanded indignantly.

Andrea laughed; she couldn't help herself. She could picture Melly's pale complexion mottled by irate splotches of pink. "No, Melly," she said in a soothing tone. "I was thinking. What time is this blast scheduled for?"

"Whenever," Melly said. "I wouldn't be surprised if some of the guys were there already."

"Oh." Andrea was quiet a moment. Then she asked, "Is everybody bringing something?" That was the way the get-togethers usually worked, every member bringing food or drink, or ice to preserve the other two.

"Sure," Melly said. "If you want to go, I can come by and pick you up. We can stop at the supermarket along the way for our contributions."

Andrea hesitated a moment longer, then would have shrugged, if she'd had the energy. "Okay, Melly. What time will you get here?"

"Say . . . forty-five minutes?"

"Say an hour," Andrea said. "Remember, I haven't

even had a cup of coffee . . . never mind breakfast."

Andrea was ready and waiting when Melly swept into the driveway in her racy sports car. A bright orange pullover and white shorts concealed the same swimsuit she had worn the day before. Thong sandals protected the soles of her feet. And, determined to avoid the necessity of an improvised fastener for her hair, she had anchored the dark mass to the back of her head with a large plastic butterfly clip.

Strangely, for reasons Andrea refused to examine, she had saved the dried and brittle piece of seaweed Paul had twined around her braid. Even as she had chided herself for doing it, she had carefully placed it in a small box in which she kept her most treasured mementos.

"Hi!" Melly greeted her as Andrea slipped into the low-slung bucket seat. "Where were you yesterday? I called you several times during the afternoon."

Andrea fastened the seat belt, then raised her trembling fingers to the back of her head. The clip was firmly in place. "I was on the beach all afternoon," she replied, flashing a smile she hoped would detract from the strain in her voice. "You should have called after dinner; I was home all evening."

Melly backed out of the driveway before answering. "I had a date." She smiled with smug satisfaction.

Andrea grasped at the opportunity to steer the conversation away from herself. "How interesting. Want to talk about it?" She already knew the answer; Melly always wanted to talk about her dates. This was no exception.

"He's wonderful." Melly sighed dramatically.

Andrea rolled her eyes, and was grateful for the concealment provided by the mirrored oversize sunglasses perched on her nose. "In what way?" she asked, again certain of the response; Melly's dates were always wonderful in every way.

"In every way." Melly sighed again, deeply.

Andrea groaned silently and was reminded of the white jacket, plastic gloves, and tooth extractor. "Would I happen to know this paragon of wonderfulness?"

Melly slanted a decidedly sly grin at her. "Prepare yourself," she said in a teasing warning. "When I tell you, it's going to blow your mind."

You're too late, Mell, somebody beat you to it, Andrea thought. "I can't wait," she said aloud.

In an obvious attempt to draw out the anticipatory tension, Melly was quiet for a moment. Then she blurted out, "It's Donald McEllevy!"

"Mac!" Andrea gaped at her friend, truly surprised. Donald—or Mac, as everyone called him—was the thirty-one-year-old member of the group. He was also the most quiet and reserved of the bunch, the complete opposite, in fact, of Melinda, who was bubbly and outgoing by nature.

"Yes, Mac." Melly's voice held a tremulous note Andrea had not heard before. "I . . . I'm in love with him." She bit her lip, then rushed on, "And it scares me, Andrea."

"Oh, Melly," Andrea murmured, reaching across the console to press a reassuring hand to her shoulder. "As you yourself said, Mac is a wonderful man. Why should being in love with him scare you?"

Melly sniffed. "Because I'm afraid it won't work." She spared a quick glance from the curving road for Andrea. "We are just so different."

Andrea could relate to Melly's feelings. An image of a tall, slender, impossibly handsome, and strangely different man drifted into her mind. Oh, boy, she thought, banishing the image. Could she ever relate to that! Repressing her own nervous and uncertain feelings, she tried to bolster her friend's morale. "I've always heard that opposites attract," she said teasingly. "Does the difference bother Mac?"

Melly giggled. "If his actions are anything to go by, I'd have to say not in the least."

"And does Mac love you?"

Melly's smile was soft. "He says he does."

Andrea was quiet a moment. Then, as Melly turned into the parking lot of the supermarket, she asked the one question that, to Andrea, was the most important in a relationship. "Do you trust him?"

Melly pulled on the hand brake, then turned to look at Andrea with eyes that held not a shadow of doubt. "Completely."

Andrea smiled and pushed her door open. "Well, then, I'd say you haven't a thing to be afraid of."

It wasn't until they were inside the store that either of the women thought to wonder what exactly they were shopping for. As she wrestled a wire cart from the clinging grip of other carts, Andrea threw out some suggestions.

"Marshmallows?"

"Uh-uh." Melly shook her head, setting her blond curls bouncing against her shoulders. "Doreen's bringing those . . . and potato chips."

Scratch the 'mallows and chips. Andrea frowned. "Pickles? Olives?"

"Mari said something about getting those," Melly murmured, perusing the shelves as they strolled along.

Andrea brought the cart to a halt at the end of the snack food aisle. "Look, at this rate, the party will be over before we get out of this store," she said in exasperation. "Suppose you tell me what you're sure some of the others are bringing, and then we'll take it from there."

Melly frowned in concentration. "Well . . . I think Janice is bringing soda, Mike said he'd pick up the beer, Dan's bringing the ice and a cooler, and Sara said she'd get the soda." She paused, then continued, "Oh, yeah, Bobby's bringing the buns, and Mac said he'd take care of the hot dogs and burgers." She raised her eyebrows. "So, what do you think?"

Andrea was thinking about crusty French bread and sharp cheese with chunks of vegetables, cool fruit salad, and a crisp white wine. "I don't know." She lifted her shoulders in a shrug. "We could take a couple of melons . . . you know, honeydew, cantaloupe, watermelon?"

"Great!" Melly agreed, veering off toward the produce department.

The section of beach where the group usually held their blasts was located close to a wide natural break in the rocky cliffs. There was ample space to park cars, and Melly deftly tooled the little sports car right in beside the open jeep that belonged to Mac.

A small, carefully confined fire crackled beneath the protective shelter of the cliffs, well back from the water's edge. A half-dozen women were busy unpacking food, stashing drinks in a large cooler chest, and spreading blankets on the sand. There wasn't a male in sight.

Amid waves and greetings, Melly looked around, scanning the terrain with a narrow-eyed gaze for Mac. A couple of the young women helped Andrea lug the melons to the cooler. Two of the others had obviously been in the ocean, as their swimsuits were wet and their hair clung to their heads.

"Where're the guys?" Melly asked.

Janice, a petite redhead, motioned toward the ocean. "In the water. They've been in there since right after we arrived." She shivered. "I think they're nuts. The water's cold."

Her eyes shaded by the sunglasses, Andrea gazed out over the water, smiling as she noticed the men engaged in male horseplay in the gently swelling waves.

"They probably don't mind the chill," she observed, suppressing a shiver as she envisioned another man braving the cold water the day before.

"I hope Mac doesn't catch a cold," Melly muttered.

Smiling at her friend's overconcern, Andrea stepped out of her shorts, pulled off her top, and settled back on one of the blankets. It was a beautiful weave, in vibrant earth colors interspersed with strips of stark white. Andrea didn't know whom the blanket belonged to, but then, it didn't matter. She was certain that the owner wouldn't object to her lying on it.

Lulled by the conversation of the young women around her, Andrea lay back and closed her eyes. Memory closed in around her, remembrances of the seemingly endless night she'd spent grappling with the unreality of the situation in which she suddenly found herself.

Fragments of memories skimmed in and out of her tired mind, the echo of a voice whispered in her ears.

"Oh, Andrea."

Had she only imagined the hunger concealed within his rough-velvet groan?

"No, Andrea. Not like this. You're too vulnerable now."

Andrea moved her head in restless discomfort. The voices of the young women were receding. What could he have meant by "Not like this" and "You're too vulnerable now"? she asked herself for the hundredth time. Unless . . . Paul could have taken her then and there— she had wanted him to take her. And he had wanted her, Andrea was positive of that. His body had betrayed him. But he had denied her and himself . . . because of her vulnerability? Had Paul been caring for her, protecting her? Not from himself, but from herself? Andrea wondered.

The idea tantalized Andrea's senses. Being cared for and protected by a man was such a novel concept, at least for Andrea, that she was not only intrigued by the speculation, she was soothed by it. But she and Paul had just met, Andrea reminded herself. Was it possible for a man to care so much for a woman he had so recently met to have protective feelings for her? As little as a day ago, Andrea would have answered herself with an unqualified no.

But then, what about her own feelings? Andrea reflected. Being terrified of sharks, yet unconcerned with her own safety, hadn't she run into the water to help him? Did her spontaneous action indicate a caring for Paul?

Yes.

For some inexplicable reason, having made the admission to herself about her feelings for Paul induced a sensation of utter relaxation in Andrea.

She was teetering on the brink of sleep when the deeper voices of the men roused her. She felt a body drop onto the blanket beside her, then went still when a soft voice spoke her name.

"Andrea?"

Paul!

Andrea's eyes flew open, and her mind went numb. She stared at him in disbelief. Had she conjured him up with her thoughts? A quick perusal of him convinced her that he was real.

His wet black curls framed his handsome face, looking as if they had been sculpted by an artist. Water glistened on his sun-burnished skin. His beautiful mouth curved into a gentle smile. And his soft, glowing blue eyes seemed to see . . . everything.

In Andrea's case, everything was the erratic beat of her heart, the unsteady rhythm of her shallow breathing, and the sudden spark of wariness in her eyes, a wariness instilled not only by her new awareness of her own feelings for him but also by her persistent uncertainty about him.

"You're afraid of me." Though his voice was pitched low, for her ears alone, Andrea glanced around to see if anyone had overheard. "Why?"

Her gaze swung back to his. Why? She swallowed. Because you swim with sharks! Because you invade my dreams! Andrea clamped her lips together to keep from answering aloud. The concepts were too weird, too wacko, to be entertained, let alone spoken out loud. Unable to endure his piercing stare, she lowered her eyes. She rubbed her hand over the smooth fiber of the blanket. "Is this yours?" she asked in a none too subtle attempt to change the subject.

"Yes, it's mine," Paul said softly.

Andrea quivered. Inside her mind, she heard his voice whisper, "As you are mine." Shaken, she glanced up quickly. He was sitting cross-legged, Indian fashion. His back was straight but not stiff, his head was tilted slightly. The warmth of his smile could have melted half of the polar region.

"You have nothing to fear from me, Andrea," he murmured. "I will never harm you."

For whatever strange reason, Andrea believed him; that frightened her even more. How could she believe, trust, a man she didn't know? Her eyes betrayed her.

Paul sighed. "It will take time, but you will understand eventually," he promised.

Andrea shook her head; she didn't know what it was he wanted her to understand; she wasn't even sure she *wanted* to know what he wanted her to understand. But she did understand one thing. Andrea recognized and understood the heat flowing swiftly through her veins; she recognized and understood the yearning urgency she felt deep within her body. The symptoms were familiar, she had felt them recently—on the afternoon she'd made love with her fantasy man in her dreams, and again yesterday afternoon on the beach. The recognition and understanding drove her off the blanket and away from him . . . to the safety of numbers among her friends.

For the remainder of the day, Andrea stayed close by at least one other person at all times. Her feelings and suspicions about Paul frightened her, but what frightened her even more was the longing she felt to be with him . . . only him.

His eyes sought her out at odd moments throughout the day, and each time they did, Andrea had to fight against an inner command to go to him. And at those times, she found herself asking the question that had tormented her through most of the night . . .

What manner of man was this?

All the others in the group accepted Paul without

question, more than accepted him; they accorded him a respect that Andrea thought bordered on adulation. It quickly became obvious to her that they didn't think he was "different," at least not in the same way she did.

He mixed well with both the men and the women. He laughed often. He never raised his voice.

Near sundown, Andrea got a few moments to talk to Melly in private while they were slicing the melons, and she casually remarked on the fact that she hadn't once heard Paul raise his voice, not even during the exuberant game of touch football the men had played before supper.

"I've known Paul a year, and I've never heard him raise his voice," Melly said, shrugging. She continued slicing a moment, then frowned. "Come to think of it, I've never seen him angry, either." She laughed. "Maybe he's not human."

Not human. Andrea shivered.

"Are you cold?" Melly asked.

Andrea managed a smile . . . a faint smile. "I felt a chill," she explained. "Maybe I got too much · sun today." Or too much Paul Hellka, she added silently.

When the last of the sun's rays drowned in the Pacific, Andrea had reason to shiver. The evening breeze wafting inland off the ocean was cool. Her shorts and sleeveless top offered little protection from the clammy nip in the air. Andrea was ready to go home, but nobody else was. Bottles of beer and soda were passed around. Andrea declined. The group began pairing off. Since she had made it clear from the beginning that she wasn't interested in pairing, Andrea was left on her own—except for Paul, who also obviously wasn't into group pairing.

She was sitting on Melly's blanket, shivering, when

Paul strolled across the sand to her. He had pulled a pair of cutoff jeans over his swim trunks and a sleeveless sweat shirt over his chest, and as far as clothes went, he looked much the same as the other guys. And yet, Paul Hellka was definitely not just one of the guys. Not by a long shot.

He was carrying his blanket in one hand and a long-necked bottle and two plastic glasses in the other. He didn't ask for permission to join her. Setting the bottle and glasses by her side, he grasped a corner of the blanket in each hand, stretched his long arm out and then, crossing his ankles, he sank fluidly to the ground beside her. He draped one arm around her trembling shoulders, giving her the warmth of the blanket and his body. Firmly tucking the other end of the blanket under his arm, he coolly proceeded to pour a golden wine into the two glasses.

"One of your favorites," he said, holding the bottle up for her inspection. "Isn't it?"

Telling herself that the only reason she didn't jump up and move away from him was because she was cold, Andrea accepted the glass and admitted, "Yes, I think I mentioned it yesterday." She didn't want to remember yesterday, but she couldn't deny the pleasure she felt knowing that he remembered.

"You've been avoiding me all day," he said, tilting his glass in a silent salute to her before testing the wine. "Delicious, you have excellent taste," he commended.

Andrea felt warm all over, and not only from the blanket. "Thank you," she replied politely. "I'm glad you like it. And, yes, I have been avoiding you," she admitted candidly, surprising herself more than him. "You . . . you make me nervous, Paul."

"But I'm making you warm as well," he murmured,

flexing his arm to draw her closer to his body. "Aren't I?"

In more ways than one, Andrea conceded, but only to herself. "I . . . ah, wanted to go home," she said, answering without actually answering. "But the others weren't ready to leave."

Paul turned to run a slow glance over the other couples, entwined beneath blankets, murmuring to each other words unclear but understood. He was smiling when he returned his gaze to Andrea. His eyes reflected the flicker of the dying fire. "Obviously," he said, laughing softly.

How old was he?

The thought sprang into Andrea's mind from out of nowhere—perhaps, she reasoned because of his tolerant attitude toward the younger group. Celia had said that his credentials were almost awesome, which indicated a more mature man. Yet Andrea had watched him surreptitiously during the afternoon, and he had played as hard as the youngest member of the crowd and had been less winded at the end of the games . . . and yet the only sustenance he took to replenish his body was a large wedge from each of the melons she and Melly had provided.

Strange, she mused, peering at him cautiously through the uncertain light provided by the low-burning flames. The other evening, Paul had seemed to be a true contemporary of Blaine's, in experience as well as in age. Yet today he appeared almost as young as Mac.

In fact, she concluded, not too happily, Paul seemed ageless.

Having already succeeded in making herself uncomfortable by the implausibility of her own thoughts, Andrea started at the low sound of Paul's voice.

"You're very quiet."

"I'm thinking."

His arm tightened around her shoulder. "Would you care to tell me what your deep thoughts are about?"

Andrea gazed at him, wondering why, since his voice held a note of teasing, she had the eerie feeling that he already knew the answer to his question. Suddenly impatient with her own wild imaginings, she said bluntly, "I was wondering about your age."

"What about it?"

Andrea gave him a wry look, but secretly appreciated his teasing. "How many years go into it?" she answered in a drawl. "Like, how old are you?"

Paul's laughter waltzed along every one of Andrea's nerve endings. "Is it important?"

Andrea was forced to wait until her senses settled before replying. "I thought only women refused to answer questions about their age," she sidestepped his question.

Paul refilled their glasses, again without spilling as much as a golden drop, before responding to her barb. "I haven't refused to answer." He smiled directly into her eyes. "I merely asked if it was important."

Tired of sparring with him, Andrea said, "Yes." Her stare dared him to continue whatever game he was playing.

"I am thirty-seven in years," Paul said softly. "And ancient in experience."

"Aren't we all?" Andrea mumbled. "I mean, ancient in experience?"

"You've been hurt by life."

It should have been a question, but it wasn't. The gentle intonation in his voice made it sound as if he had no need to ask the question, because he already knew that answer.

"And I don't want to talk about it," Andrea said, scrambling away from him and jumping up. She'd had just about enough of his insight or intuition, or whatever it was that was making her feel so damned odd!

Paul didn't try to coax her back. He didn't say a word. He just watched as she stood there, looking around. Andrea took two steps, and then stopped. She didn't have the heart—or the nerve—to interrupt the others. She sighed, then reluctantly turned to look at him.

"I'm tired, Paul," she said. "Will you take me home?"

As if "tired" was the magic word, Paul sprang to his feet. "Of course," he said, slinging the blanket over his arm. "All you had to do was ask."

Andrea didn't bother making the rounds of the blanket-shrouded couples to say good night, she figured they probably wouldn't hear her if she did. But Paul searched out Mac and Melly. There was a murmured exchange; then he returned to her. After collecting her beach bag, Andrea followed him to the parking area. Her eyes widened when he led her to Mac's open jeep.

"I came with Mac," he explained.

"You told Melly you were taking me home?"

"Yes." Paul helped her into the high seat. "Here"— he wrapped the blanket around her—"you'll need this."

The rather loud sound of the jeep's engine limited all but a few shouted words between them during the short drive to Celia's house. Andrea was glad; she felt out of conversation—and completely out of her depth.

Not waiting for his assistance, she leaped from the vehicle the minute he brought it to a stop in the driveway. "Thanks for the lift," she said, cringing inwardly at the timid schoolgirl sound of her voice.

"You're welcome," Paul replied in a tone rife with suppressed laughter.

"You're laughing at me," Andrea accused him.

"Yes." Stepping out of the driver's seat, Paul strolled to where she was hovering uncertainly on the other side of the jeep. Raising his hand, he stroked the curve of her jawline with his fingertips. "I can't resist." Lowering his head, he brushed his mouth over hers, then captured her lips in a whisper-light kiss.

It was only after Paul had walked her to the door, whispered good night, and left that Andrea thought to wonder whether it was laughing at her or kissing her that he found so difficult to resist.

Chapter Seven

IT WAS THE FIRST day of classes of the fall semester. Five days had passed, crawled, dragged by since the beach party, and since Andrea had seen Paul. But he had invaded her thoughts throughout every moment of every one of those five days.

On the surface Andrea appeared normal. She had returned to work at the boutique. She had spent an evening in Monterey with Celia and Blaine. She had whiled away an entire afternoon shopping for fall clothes with Melly, after which they had met two other women from the group for a pizza supper and a movie. She had had her hair trimmed. And she had enjoyed every one of the normal activities . . . to all outward appearances.

Inside, however, the real Andrea was in a state of disorganization and confusion. As she had suspected, after that last dream she'd had of him waving farewell, her fantasy man had not returned to her. Andrea's imaginary lover no longer came to her in her sleep. Her nights were peaceful, but in her waking hours Andrea was never completely alone.

When she was in the company of others—her aunt, Blaine, her friends, or customers and co-workers in the small specialty shop—Paul lounged at the edges of her consciousness, never interfering, content to keep her constantly aware of his presence with his soft smile and compassionate eyes.

When she was alone, Paul made his presence felt with whispering echoes of every word he had spoken to her and with visions of every moment they had spent together.

In effect, since the beach party, Andrea had not known one solitary moment.

Paul Hellka haunted her mind.

In a way Andrea found impossible to comprehend, it was as if, by design, Paul had taken over where her fantasy lover had left off. It didn't make any kind of sense, and yet a suspicion grew within her that Paul and her imaginary lover were one and the same man.

But, Andrea asked herself, if her expanding suspicions about Paul were true, how had he accomplished the feat of mental invasion?

Telepathy?

Andrea considered the obvious, rational explanation. Were there not documented cases of telepathic communication? And hadn't her aunt and just about everyone else who knew him told her that Paul was considered brilliant to the degree of awesome?

Yes, and yes, Andrea answered herself. But, she immediately argued silently, were there any documented cases of telepathy powerful enough not only to intrude upon but to manipulate another's unconscious, dreaming self? Could any telepathic mind be so awesomely powerful?

Positive that, if the scientific community had ever encountered a mind that powerful, the news media would have exploited the discovery worldwide, Andrea had to reject the possibility. As far as she knew, the ability of one mind to project itself into the sleeping, dreaming mind of another was beyond the capability of the human intellect.

It was at this point in Andrea's mental scramblings that Melly's casual remark returned to taunt her.

"Maybe the man's not human."

And it was at this point that Andrea had dismissed her suspicions as the spawn of her own longings. In simple terms, she unconsciously *wanted* Paul and her dream lover to be one and the same man.

It was the only answer that didn't leave Andrea wondering if her mental wrappings were beginning to fray.

Andrea seriously considered flight, back to the safe, if unexciting, life she was familiar with, A life that excluded male companionship. A life as empty and barren as her body.

Would her fantasy man return to her in her dreams if she distanced herself from Paul? she wondered. Or would she be missing out on the chance of a lifetime by throwing away the opportunity to get to know him?

Andrea pondered her choices throughout every one of those five days between the beach party and the first day of classes for the fall semester.

In the end, Andrea decided that she was finished with hiding herself, her real self, from men in general, and from Paul Hellka in particular.

Paul interested her . . . No, her feelings ran deeper

than interest: She cared for him . . . No, her feelings ran even deeper than caring. She . . .

That was as far as Andrea ever allowed her thoughts to delve. She wasn't sure exactly what it was she felt for him, but she had determined to explore those feelings.

The not-so-intrepid explorer approached the first of her earth studies classes arrayed in the material armor of one of her new outfits and the spiritual armor of skepticism.

The student body at Parker was small and select, and so there were less than a dozen students gathered in the lecture hall. Accustomed to throngs of students and overcrowded classrooms, Andrea was amazed and delighted with the limited size of all her classes.

Although this was the last class of the day, an anticipatory excitement still hummed on the air. Greetings were called back and forth between students who hadn't seen each other all summer. Animated conversation and laughter bounced off the somber wood-paneled walls.

Being a part of the class, and yet separate as a new member, Andrea relaxed and enjoyed listening to the boisterous exchanges of fraternity and goodwill. In truth, it sounded like bedlam. Then a low-pitched, calm voice sliced through the noise and brought an immediate silence to the hall.

"Shall we begin?"

Andrea hadn't seen Paul enter the hall. Like every other student in the room, she sat up straight in her chair and gave him her undivided attention.

Dressed casually in neatly pressed slacks and a short-sleeved shirt, unbuttoned at the throat, Paul was standing loose-limbed beside a large desk in the front of the room. His tousled black hair had the look of having won a battle against a vigorously applied brushing.

For Andrea, the sight of him, after five endless days of deliberately avoiding him, was like the sight of a lavish banquet to a starving person. Every particle of her body, mind, and soul hungered for him. Her senses were attuned to the slightest nuance of his voice.

"Welcome to the earth," he said in opening. "I am Professor Hellka, and I will be your guide to the abundant wonders the earth and nature have to offer."

Andrea was enthralled. In four years of college, she had attended many first classes taught by an equal number of professors, yet never had she heard a more intriguing introduction to any subject. Before the class was half over, Andrea had reached the conclusion that Paul was not merely brilliant but an absolute genius of a teacher. And the truly amazing part was that he did it so effortlessly.

He would toss an idea into the minds of his rapt audience and invite open discussion. Then through the give-and-take of intelligent discourse would emerge clarity of the subject.

As inspired as every other member of the class, Andrea joined in on all the discussions, at times taking exception to a comment Paul had tossed into the animated debate. At these times, he would single her out with his eyes, sending her silent messages of warm approval while they argued the point.

They were in the middle of one such argument, concerning atmosphere in relation to space travel, when the class ended. Her fellow students sat quietly while she finished stating her position. His dark eyes reflecting the late afternoon sunlight slanting through the long, narrow windows in the west wall of the lecture hall, Paul skimmed a smiling glance over the assemblage.

"Thank you for your participation, ladies and gentlemen," he said, dismissing the class. There was an immediate rustle and shuffle of movement.

Feeling let down and disappointed, Andrea closed her notebook and collected her belongings. His soft voice froze her in place as she was preparing to stand.

"Miss Trask, if you care to remain, I will be happy to correct the error in your argument."

Andrea hesitated a moment and then, reminding herself of her resolution to get to know him better, she settled back again in her chair.

With freedom beckoning, the other students left the hall as swiftly as if someone had yelled fire. When only she and Paul were left, Andrea looked into his eyes, and completely forgot the subject of their disagreement.

His long legs swallowed the distance separating them. "It's too nice to remain indoors," he said as he approached her. "Will you walk with me?"

Without a word, Andrea stood, gathered her books together, and preceded him from the hall. The sun was warm, the air sparkling. In silence, she followed his lead. Since she really didn't care where he was heading, she didn't bother to ask. She was content to stroll by his side.

Paul didn't chide her for avoiding him or for her failure to return his calls over the past five days. He didn't refer to classroom subject matter, either. In fact, he didn't speak at all until they had left the campus and entered a grove of tangy-scented pine trees off to one side of the college buildings.

Coming to a sudden halt, Paul turned to look at her. Dappled sunlight played over his handsome face, highlighting the perfection of his features. His blue eyes had the depth of the ocean and seemed to hold the wisdom of the ages. "I've missed you," he said in that soft tone Andrea now realized was natural to him.

She briefly considered evasion, then discarded the idea as detrimental to her purpose. "I've missed you, too," she replied in a tone as soft as his own.

"And yet you didn't return my calls." There wasn't a hint of censure in his voice, only patience and compassion.

Andrea lowered her eyes. "I was afraid," she admitted.

"Of me?"

She caught her bottom lip between her teeth. Could she go through with it? Andrea asked herself. Could she really say the words that would expose the woman hiding behind her protective facade? Her parched throat sent forth a dry whisper. "No, I was afraid of me."

"Oh, Andrea." Paul took one step toward her, then stopped. "I want to touch you," he said, caressing her with his eyes. "I want to kiss you." He inhaled sharply, as if drawing in strength. Then he smiled. "But I can't . . . not yet."

Andrea felt an inner warmth that had nothing to do with the sunshine, and an outer chill that had nothing to do with the shade. "Why—" She paused to moisten her dry lips; his deep blue eyes followed the movement of her tongue. His intent gaze caused a shiver to tingle down her spine, and she had to concentrate to remember what she'd started to ask. "Why not?"

"You're not ready," he said. "Are you?"

Yes! The word leaped into her mind. "No," she answered, knowing it was the only answer she could give him.

"I thought not." Paul's smile held acceptance and tolerant amusement. "You're afraid to trust me."

Though he hadn't posed it as a question, Andrea nodded in answer. "I don't know you, Paul."

"You do, you know," he murmured. "You know me on your deepest level—intuitively. But you don't trust your intuition, either. Do you?"

"No," Andrea answered in a flat tone, recalling the pain she had suffered once before after trusting her intuition. "I had to learn the hard way that my feelings can betray me. Since then, I've relied on my reasoning faculties."

"And your mind can't betray you?" Paul asked gently.

Andrea felt trapped. She couldn't admit to him of all people that until a few days ago she had trusted her reasoning mind implicitly. Nor could she tell him that, because of him, she was no longer certain of anything, not even her own mind. "Perhaps it can," she said, circumventing the issue. "Nevertheless, until I know you better . . ." Her voice trailed off and she shrugged.

"Since you won't even return my calls," he observed, a teasing challenge glittering in his eyes, "how do you propose to get to know me better?"

"I'm here," Andrea said. "Aren't I?"

"Yes, you are here." Paul smiled. "And we have made a beginning." With a resolute move, he turned and started back the way they had come into the grove. "Let's see where this beginning leads us."

Andrea hesitated a moment, then struck out after him. She was committed now. Or, she mused, increasing her stride to keep up with him, maybe she *should* be committed.

When they were once again on campus and able to walk side by side, Paul tilted his head and smiled at her.

"And when does this exploration into my psyche begin?"

"You just said it had begun," Andrea countered.

Paul laughed.

Andrea felt herself melting.

"Then, when can it continue?"

Andrea frowned. "Why, I don't know . . . When do you—"

"Dinner?" Paul interjected.

"This evening?" Anticipation zinged through Andrea.

"Yes, this evening." Paul raised his eyebrows. "Okay?"

Andrea hesitated . . . only because she didn't want to appear too eager. "Yes."

"Seven? Six-thirty? . . . Six?"

Andrea interrupted him with a laugh. "Six-thirty will be fine for me."

Paul's eyes seemed to take on an added gleam. "And I hope to prove that I will be fine for you, too."

His softly voiced hope sang in Andrea's head as she drove to the cliff house. She was still confused by his uncanny resemblance to her dream lover, and still convinced that there was something strange about him, but she was more determined than before to solve the mystery surrounding him. Andrea knew that she had no other choice, for she was very much afraid that she was falling in love with Paul Hellka.

Celia was delighted. "It's about time you came out of that shell you've built around yourself," she said in a caring, parental tone. Then she grinned. "You don't want to be an old spinster like me, do you?"

"Aunt Celia, I'm going to dinner; I'm not planning to elope!" Andrea exclaimed on a burst of laughter. "And if Blaine has his head on straight . . . which I believe he does . . . you won't be a spinster much longer."

Celia grew flushed and flustered, which in itself was telling. Celia never flushed or became flustered.

"Are you keeping something from me?" Andrea asked suspiciously.

For a moment, Celia hesitated. Then she said, "As a matter of fact, Blaine has asked me to marry him."

"You said yes, I hope," Andrea said, and gave her aunt a hug.

"Well . . . not exactly," Celia hedged.

"Not exactly!" Andrea cried. "Aunt Celia, you're crazy about Blaine! I don't understand why you'd hesitate." Her eyes narrowed as an idea hit her. "Your hesitation doesn't have anything to do with me, does it?"

"Andrea, Blaine hasn't only asked me to marry him," Celia said. "He is taking a sabbatical for a year. He hasn't had a real vacation in ages, and he wants to do some traveling before he's too old or too tired to enjoy it."

"Makes sense to me," Andrea said. "So . . . ?"

"His leave starts on the first of October. He wants me to marry him and go with him on his travels." Celia paused, then went on, "I don't want to leave you here on your own."

"But I'm twenty-eight years old and perfectly capable of looking after myself!" Andrea objected.

"I know that," Celia replied. "But you've been fighting an uphill battle by yourself for so long now"—her smile was misty—"I just wanted to be here for you."

"Oh, Aunt Celia." Andrea blinked against the sting of tears in her eyes. "I love you and I appreciate your concern, but you see, through all those rough years, I always knew you were there for me, even though you were three thousand miles away." Celia tried to say something, but Andrea shook her head. "Don't let Blaine go away alone. Marry him. Be deliriously happy traipsing around the world with him, because, don't you see, distance can never truly separate us."

They cried together, hugged each other, then laughed as they drew apart.

"You're right, of course," Celia said, handing Andrea a tissue. "I'll tell Blaine I'll marry him . . . maybe this evening over dinner."

"Dinner!" Andrea cried, swinging around to glance at the clock. "I've got to take a shower and dress!"

"Wear something terrific and blow his mind away," Celia called laughingly as Andrea dashed for her bedroom.

The something terrific Andrea finally settled on—after changing her mind, and her dress, three times—was a deceptively simple silk sheath in teal blue that clung like ivy to her slender body and shimmered with iridescent highlights with every move she made. She complemented the dress with sling-heeled sandals and a shawl that looked as if it had been woven out of misty moonbeams.

Andrea's fingers shook as she smoothed silvery shadow on her eyelids, finishing off her makeup with a touch of moisturizer, a swish of blusher, and a sweep of mascara. With a liberal spray of jasmine scent, she declared herself ready.

Surveying her reflection in the mirror, Andrea decided she looked cool, composed, and pretty good over all. Inside, she was a quivering mass of uncertainty.

The expression that flickered over Paul's face when she entered the living room at precisely six-thirty was more than enough reward for her painstaking efforts.

While he didn't exactly look blown away, he did appear slightly stunned.

Andrea recognized the condition, for she was feeling rather dazed herself. With his tall, slim body attired in a midnight-blue suit and a pale blue shirt, Paul was the embodiment of elegance.

"Utterly beautiful," he breathed as she crossed the room to him. "But then, you always are."

Bemused, Andrea whispered, "You're beautiful, too."

His soft laughter was echoed by the two other people in the room. Her eyes flickering with surprise, Andrea spun around. She had completely forgotten that Celia and Blaine were in the house. "I . . . er, didn't see you two," she admitted, feeling her cheeks grow warm with embarrassment.

"Obviously," Celia drawled. "But that's understandable. Paul *is* somewhat blinding, isn't he?"

Blaine laughed. "Actually, they are both somewhat blinding, if you ask me. Talk about beautiful people!"

"I think this is their unsubtle way of telling us we look good together," Paul said, holding out his hand to Andrea. "Shall we go and blind the world?"

Laughing with him, she slid her hand into his, said good night to Celia and Blaine, then followed him outside. Since this was the first time she had seen it, his car was a surprise. It was silver, low, sleek and, Andrea suspected, custom-built. She had never seen anything like it before.

"This is fantastic!" Andrea exclaimed after they were ensconced in the plush leather seats. "What is it, and where did you find it?"

"It doesn't have a name," Paul replied, smiling as he

reached forward to switch on the engine. "And I didn't find it. I built it."

"Incredible," Andrea whispered in amazement.

The sound of Paul's laughter blended with the powerful purr of the engine. "Buckle up," he advised as he drove onto the road. "I drive fast."

That was the ultimate understatement, Andrea decided, after what seemed a short zoom to the restaurant. Only later did she realize that, although Paul had driven at a speed she didn't even wish to think about, she had not experienced a moment of anxiety or fear.

The restaurant was secluded, the lighting was subdued, the cuisine was superb. Andrea barely noticed. Her senses were saturated by the man seated opposite her at the small table next to a large window.

They spoke little, they ate less, they sipped a flavorful white wine.

And Paul made love to her with his eyes.

When they left the restaurant, Andrea couldn't remember tasting what she had eaten, although she had a vague recollection of a creamy cold soup and a cheesy pasta entrée. The wine bubbled through her veins.

From the restaurant Paul drove to a smoky little tavern where the service was fast and the music was slow. There, oblivious to the other patrons, Andrea lost her heart while dancing in Paul's arms. His hands caressed her spine, his lips brushed her temple, his lean body pressed to hers set her on fire. She wanted him, and the wanting scared her.

Paul sensed her withdrawal the instant she advised herself to cool her emotions. Easing his head back, he gazed into her eyes. A smile shadowed by sadness tinged his beautiful mouth. "You want to run away from me now," he murmured, skillfully moving her closer to the edge of the small dance floor. "Don't you?"

Andrea lowered her lashes to conceal her eyes, unwilling to let him see her inner battle between conflicting emotions. "Yes, I . . . I would like to go home now. If you don't mind?"

"I wouldn't mind at all—in fact, I'd be thrilled—if you wanted to go to your *real* home."

Andrea's lashes swept up, revealing the confusion she was feeling about his enigmatic response. "Paul, I don't understand what you're—"

"It doesn't matter," he interrupted her. "You'll understand before too long." Without another word, he led her out to his car. He didn't speak again until they were on the road. "You were frightened of your feelings back there, weren't you?" he asked astutely.

Andrea was beginning to feel trapped again. "Paul, I still don't know you," she said in a tight whisper. "One evening spent together isn't enough to warrant—" Andrea faltered, unable to finish aloud—*spending the night together*.

"I know. It's all right." His soft sigh filled the silence inside the car. "I understand."

They were quiet during the drive to the cliff house, and quiet as he saw her to the door. When he moved to draw her into his arms, Andrea placed her hand on his chest. "I need more time, Paul." Her voice held a note of pleading. "Time to get to know you."

Paul let his arms fall to his sides, then stepped back. "Very well, Andrea. I can wait . . . a little longer." Raising his hand, he trailed his fingertips over her mouth. "Tomorrow afternoon after class?" he asked.

"Yes," Andrea whispered on an uneven breath. "Tomorrow afternoon."

The following afternoon set a precedent for several

weeks to come. When the weather permitted, they walked together, at times arguing a point raised in the classroom, at others simply talking. When the weather was inclement, they sat over steaming cups of coffee in various cafés, or visited marine or natural history museums, and did exactly the same thing—talked and argued. Through it all, Andrea discovered many things about Paul's professional life, and her admiration and respect for him grew with each passing day. But she learned very little about the man himself, the inner person who was Paul Hellka.

Then, on a beautiful warm day in late September, everything changed. As had become her habit, Andrea was waiting for Paul outside the lecture hall. Everything seemed as usual. When Paul came out of the building, he reached for her hand.

"Good class today," Andrea complimented him, sliding her hand into his.

Paul sent a mini-thrill through her with his slow smile, which began on his mouth and ended in his fascinating eyes. "Thank you. You do your part to keep things lively." Twining his fingers with hers, he began walking.

"Where are we going today?" she asked, falling into step with him. She arched her brows teasingly. "To the beach to examine tide pools for squiggly things?"

Paul's smile slid into a grin. "It's an idea. We haven't done that yet." He shook his head. "But, no, not today. I have something, a place, to show you."

Intrigued, Andrea strolled beside him. She began to frown when he headed for the copse of pine trees they'd walked into on the first day of classes. "But we've been here before, Paul," she reminded him. "Don't you remember?"

"I remember everything that has anything at all to do with you, Andrea," he replied seriously. Retaining his hold on her hand, he stepped out in front of her to lead the way into the dense pine thicket. "I wanted to show this place to you that day," he went on. "But you weren't ready to see it." Pausing, he turned to look at her. "I think, I hope, that you are now comfortable enough with me to go with me." Appearing to cease breathing, he watched her in absolute stillness, waiting for her response.

All the tension, which had eased in her over the weeks they'd spent talking and laughing together, slammed back into Andrea. Not once during those weeks had Paul pressured her in any way. Now Andrea knew the pressure, however delicate, was being applied, and she hesitated.

She swallowed; he noted the action.

She moistened her lips; his eyes darkened.

She asked herself if she was truly ready; he waited for her answer.

Moments stretched into minutes. Then, managing a smile for him, she gave in. "All right, Paul. Take me to this place you want me to see."

"Ahh . . . Andrea." Paul's low voice revealed a wealth of emotions, the strongest of which was relief. Reaching out, he grasped her hand. Entwining her fingers with his, he tugged gently on her hand and murmured, "Come."

His whisper was both a plea and a command. A chord was struck deep inside Andrea. She had heard him say that word before, in exactly that tone, but . . . when? It was too late. There wasn't time for her to sift through her memory bank. After turning away, Paul was drawing her with him, deeper into the pine thicket.

The elusive scent of the sea, mingled with the pungent tang of pine, assailed Andrea's senses as they came out of the pine grove. It was then that she saw the pathway.

A sensation of uneasiness uncurled inside Andrea. The terrain beyond the edge of the grove seemed familiar. Yet she knew she had never been there before. Her uneasiness growing with each successive step, Andrea tightened her fingers around his, clinging to his hand as if to a lifeline.

The path was barely wide enough for them to walk side by side. With every step she took, Andrea felt a growing familiarity and a deepening unease.

The trees began to thin out, then became sparse on the uneven landscape. Andrea's breathing grew shallow. Her palm grew moist against his.

"Paul?" Her voice was little more than a raspy whisper, as he drew her into a grassy clearing shaded by an ancient tree with a gnarled trunk.

His hand tightened around hers. "I am here, my heart," he murmured. "You have nothing to fear."

The sweet, cherished familiarity of his voice, his words, in this place, was too much to bear.

Andrea's last thought before she lost consciousness was that she had walked, wide awake, into her own dream.

Chapter Eight

WHEN ANDREA REGAINED CONSCIOUSNESS she was lying on a cushion of soft grass, gently cradled in Paul's strong embrace. Her head was resting on his chest. His fingers were lightly brushing her temple.

"Who are you?" Her voice was thin and colorless. Turning in his arms, she stared into his eyes. "Who are you?" she demanded with more strength.

His eyes glowed from within with compassion and . . . more. "I am exactly who I said I was—Paul Hellka."

"I'm going mad!" Andrea cried, struggling to break free of his hold.

"No, you're not." His arms held her fast.

Unable to free herself, Andrea lay still and closed her eyes. "I don't understand any of this!" Her eyes opened wide as a suspicion crept into her mind, a suspicion about him and her dream lover and this clearing. "Why did you bring me here? How did you know about this place?"

"This spot is not very far from Parker," he pointed out, indicating the area with a negligent gesture of his hand. "I've been coming here every day since I arrived in California. I pass by here as I walk between my home and the college," he explained. "And this place was not my destination today. I wanted you to see my home."

Andrea felt more confused than ever. "Your home?" she repeated. "You live near here?"

"Yes. Within walking distance."

"I see," she said. But Andrea didn't see. She didn't see anything but the compelling lure of his eyes. Afraid she'd drown in the depths of his dark blue eyes, she glanced away, to stare at the lighter blue sky through the twisted branches of the old tree. Memory stirred and brought tears to her eyes. "Why did you call me 'my heart'?"

"Because you are my heart." He drew a shiver to her skin by brushing his lips from her temple to the corner of her mouth. "Oh, Andrea, after all this time, don't you know? Can't you feel my heart beating for you . . . only for you?"

"Paul . . ." Andrea turned her head; his mouth covered hers.

"My heart," he whispered against her lips.

His touch was both new and familiar. Vibrantly awake, yet lost in a dream, Andrea sighed and gave her mouth to him, once more reliving the wonder of his kiss.

His mouth did not make demands, but sweetly, delicately explored the contours of hers. Andrea felt the thrill of a promise of possession. He was hers again, her love.

Reality returned with a cold rush when Paul withdrew his mouth from hers. The warm tears escaped the confines of her eyelids and slowly trickled over her temples and into her hair.

Paul caught one tear with his lips. "Why do you weep, when we are at last together?" he murmured.

"I don't know. I'm not sure." Andrea turned her face into his chest. "Oh, Paul," she sobbed, "I'm not sure of anything anymore!"

"You can be sure of me," he said. "Trust me."

"I can't." Andrea moved her head and heard the steady beat of his heart. "I want to, but I can't. Not yet." She felt his chest expand, then contract in a sigh.

"My poor Andrea," he said, caressing her face with feather-light kisses. "I wish I could resolve the confusion in your mind, but I can't . . . not yet, not until you are free enough to trust yourself and me implicitly."

With a sigh, Andrea realized that in his usual calm, compassionate way, Paul had pinpointed the very core of her problem. She was more afraid to trust herself, her intuition, her feelings for and about him, than she was to trust him. The facade she had created out of the pain of betrayal had settled and become permanent. Discarding that protective shield and exposing her inner self would require a strength and courage Andrea wasn't sure she possessed.

Afraid that she might never be able to summon up that much strength, Andrea looked at him, tears shimmering in her hazel eyes. "Oh, Paul, what are we going to do?" she cried, in her fear unaware that her use of the word "we" revealed to him the tiny cracks already undermining her facade. "I feel like such a coward."

"You are no more a coward than you are mad," Paul said in that soft tone she was becoming addicted to.

"And we will go on as before. There is still time."

Andrea didn't understand his last remark, but that wasn't unusual; she really didn't comprehend half of what he said to her. Mentally clinging to his assurance, she literally clung to the reassuring strength of his body. "I want to let go of the fear, Paul," she said. "I want to be free of it . . ." Andrea hesitated, then confessed, "I want to be with you."

Paul closed his eyes, as if gathering fortitude. His arms tightened almost compulsively around her slender form. "We will be together, as we have been," he murmured. "But from now on we will be together here, in our special place, where we can express our thoughts and feelings in private." His kiss was as soft, and as addictive, as his voice.

Bemused, Andrea sighed. "I've always loved this place," she said, unaware of what she was revealing to him.

"So have I," he replied. "This is the perfect place for us to meet."

And so, throughout the days that followed, Andrea found herself living a parallel of her dreams.

Some days they would meet after class and walk to the clearing together. On other days, when Paul was detained by meetings, Andrea would go to the clearing alone and wait for him. And there were days when, due to the bustle of activity surrounding her aunt's approaching wedding, Andrea would arrive late at the clearing. As in her dreams, he was always there, on the path, waiting for her.

And slowly, as the days slipped by, Andrea began to release the fears, insecurities, and inhibitions chaining her to memories of pain and betrayal.

Paul was patient, always willing to follow her lead
. . . in conversation and in caresses.

"Oh, Paul, wait till you see Aunt Celia's dress!" Andrea exclaimed one rain-misted early evening. It was
mid-October, and the days were growing short—in
daylight and in the time left before Celia's wedding.
"She looks beautiful and young and . . . so gloriously
happy," she continued.

Paul's eyes examined her glowing face, and a tender
smile curved his mouth. "Celia's in love," he said simply. Then he laughed. "But have you noticed the change
in Blaine since your aunt agreed to marry him?" When
she nodded in response, he went on, "Blaine is like a
different man . . ." He paused, then continued meaning-
fully, "The emptiness inside Blaine seems to have been
filled by the love he and Celia share."

"You don't think it's silly?" Andrea asked, recalling
that she'd overheard one of the older professors saying
rather cynically that Blaine was so besotted he was
making a fool of himself.

Paul frowned. "Silly? I don't know what you mean."

Andrea briefly related to him what she had overheard, then added, "You know, most men think it's only
women who get all mushy about love."

"And most men never know what it is that's missing
from their dreary lives," Paul concluded for her. "No,
Andrea, I do not think Blaine's behavior is silly. I think
it's wonderful that he has found in Celia the woman
who completes his life. I am happy for Blaine, and I'm
proud that he has asked me to share his joy by being his
best man at the ritual joining them as husband and
wife."

Surprised and somewhat dazed by his response, Andrea stared up at Paul in utter fascination while a familiar question skipped through her mind.

What manner of man was this?

During the preceding weeks, Andrea had begun to understand what manner of man Paul was. She now knew him to be a very complex personality. He was brilliant—yet he never acted superior. And his brilliance extended far beyond his chosen field of earth science. His knowledge of history, technology, the arts, and the other sciences was astounding. In his day-to-day dealings with people, he revealed a nature that was compassionate, tolerant, understanding, and humorous. And, as Melly had indicated weeks ago, Andrea had yet to see him display anger.

And yet, with all the facets of his personality that Andrea had come to recognize as uniquely Paul's, she had the strangest feeling that as many facets were still unrevealed to her. So, in effect, Andrea did not know what manner of man Paul Hellka really was.

But there was now one very major difference in Andrea's confusion concerning Paul. Instead of reacting with suspicion to this extraordinary man, Andrea found him even more intriguing and exciting.

"Aunt Celia told me your parents were immigrants," Andrea said one warm, lazy Sunday afternoon, finally expressing her curiosity about his family.

They were lounging beneath the old tree, almost exactly the way they had in her dreams. Paul's back was propped against the gnarled trunk, and Andrea was cradled between his thighs, her head resting on the breathing pillow of his chest. She felt his laughter rumble through his chest before it erupted into the mild autumn air.

"I thought you'd never raise that subject," he murmured, idly stroking the back of her hand with one finger. "Actually, Celia is only half correct."

"Half correct?" Andrea repeated, absently returning his light caress by drawing circles on his arm with one fingernail. "Which half?"

"My mother was born in this country," he explained. "My father was an"—his pause was barely noticeable —"illegal alien," he finished softly.

"Illegal!" Andrea exclaimed, twisting around to stare at him in surprise. "Do you mean he entered this country without permission?"

Paul's mouth twitched with an inner amusement that Andrea was at a loss to comprehend, considering the seriousness of the subject.

"Oh, most assuredly without permission," he said, his somber tone at odds with the laughter glittering in his eyes. "He crossed the border into this country in the Big Bend area of Texas," he added.

Her mind occupied by thoughts of the numbers of oppressed people who had sought freedom by crossing the Rio Grande, Andrea didn't notice the slight emphasis he'd placed on the word "border." "Umm," she murmured. "I understand that many aliens enter this country in that section of Texas."

"Yes," he agreed, still in that amused tone. "Many more than most people imagine."

Andrea barely heard his words, let alone the laughter woven through them. All her attention was centered on the sensations being sparked deep inside her by the slow, sensuous glide of his hand from her waist to her shoulder. A tingle in her palm brought her to the awareness of her own hand concurrently stroking the outside of his thigh.

"Paul?" she whispered achingly when his fingers delicately probed the hollow at the base of her throat.

"What is it, my heart?" he murmured, as his fingers drifted beneath the collar of her silk shirt to examine the delicate curve of her shoulder. "Tell me what you're feeling," he said softly. "Deep down, inside yourself."

Her hand slowly moved to the front of his taut thigh. "Warm," she breathed. "And protected and . . ."

"Yes?" he urged her to finish.

"Cherished." Her breath whispered through her parted lips, mingling with his as he lowered his mouth to hers.

"You are all of those," he murmured into her mouth. "I will keep you warm and protected and cherished for as long as breath and life quicken your body."

Stirred deeply by his promise, Andrea raised her hand to his face to draw his mouth to hers.

This time his kiss was different. His mouth moved over hers in hungry exploration. His lips were hard with restrained passion. His tongue tasted the sweetness of her mouth with infinite tenderness.

Warmth suffused Andrea's body, arousing her senses, clouding her mind. Needing to be closer to him, she turned completely in his embrace to lie against him, their bodies aligned. Her breasts ached, and seeking relief, she moved sensuously against his chest. Without conscious direction, her hand glided to the curve of his slim hips, her fingers flexed, digging into the soft denim of his jeans. Striving to touch as much of his body with her own as possible, she arched her spine like a bow, unaware of the discomfort of her unnatural position.

Paul was made aware of it as he slid his hand the length of her spine. His hand came to a stop at her waist and was joined by his other hand to gently lift her up and away from him. Andrea moaned a protest as her mouth was lifted from his.

"Wait, my heart," he whispered. "You will injure yourself this way." Revealing a strength Andrea wouldn't have believed possible for any man, he gripped her waist and lifted her bodily away from him, into the air.

Stunned into absolute stillness, Andrea could only watch in amazement as he held her aloft above him, while simultaneously easing his body away from the tree and onto the grass-cushioned ground. Then, smiling into her shock-widened eyes, he slowly lowered his arms and settled her gently on his body.

Andrea's rattled thoughts tumbled over one another as they skipped through her mind. She had witnessed incredible feats of strength before, performed by weightlifters and the like. Nevertheless, she would not have believed it possible for a man to accomplish the feat Paul had just performed.

She was five feet nine inches in height and weighed 130 pounds! And, though Paul stood close to six feet six, he was slender to the point of slim, and leanly muscled! Yet he had not only held her in the air above him but had shifted his body from his lounging position against the tree into a prone position on the floor of the clearing!

Surely what he had just done was physically impossible! Andrea's rational mind insisted. It had to be some sort of trick, an illusion, she reasoned, even though she had been suspended in midair, supported entirely by his physical strength.

"How did you do that?" Andrea asked in a voice made hoarse by both suspicion and awe.

Paul laughed and settled her more comfortably on top

of his body. "Mind over matter," he said jokingly.

Unconvinced, Andrea frowned at him in consternation. "It's really a trick, isn't it?" she said skeptically. "A magician's illusion."

"Is it?" Paul's soft voice was rich with laughter. "In that case," he went on, "since your sensual mood has obviously been cooled by disruptive thoughts, I'll give you a repeat performance." His lips twitched. "An encore."

Andrea began to shake her head slowly. "I don't think . . . Paul!" It was too late for her protest; he had commenced his encore.

Grasping her again by the waist, he lifted her high in the air, away from his body, and slowly arched his spine. Then, just as Andrea feared she would hear his spine snap, he catapulted himself up from the ground, taking her with him. When he was standing upright, Paul lowered her to her feet.

"Did you like that trick, my Andrea?"

"I don't believe this!" Andrea exclaimed in a shocked whisper. "You're not even winded!"

It was true. Paul was breathing normally, and he didn't seem to have exerted himself at all. Feeling weak all over and trembly inside, Andrea stared at him in mute appeal. Intellectually, she knew there had been no trickery involved in his demonstration of strength. Rationally, she knew the feat he'd performed was every bit as impossible as swimming safely with sharks. Yet she had witnessed both feats with her own eyes . . . and had been a participant in one of them.

"Are you now preparing to run away from me, as you did that day on the beach?"

Had Paul read her mind? Or were her thoughts and emotions written on her expressive face? Andrea mused, pondering the sudden realization that it no longer mattered to her, either way. He was different from other men...Boy, was he different! The difference made no difference to her.

"No, I'm not preparing to run," she replied, still shaken, but managing a smile for him. "I think you're a little strange, Paul...No, I think you're a lot strange," she said candidly. Then she shrugged. "But that doesn't bother me anymore. In fact, I rather like your strangeness."

His laughter started low, then built into a joyful sound that danced merrily on the sea-scented air. Once again he grasped her by the waist, this time to swing her off her feet and into a crushing embrace.

"We're almost there, my Andrea," he said, lowering his head to hers. "We're almost there."

Andrea might have asked him where "there" was, if she hadn't gotten lost within a world where thought was not necessary—a world created by the pressure of his mouth on hers.

Their kiss was long and deep and mutually satisfying. When he raised his head to look at her, Andrea didn't even think to conceal her desire from him.

"Ah...my Andrea," he murmured. "I could happily die knowing that you are, at last, mine for the taking. But I won't." His mouth curved into a smile both sensuous and teasing. "I'm going to live to make glorious, passionate love to you for a very long time...perhaps as long as two or three hundred years."

Feeling light, free, completely unfettered by the past and her own fears, Andrea laughed. "You're not only strange, Paul Hellka, you're crazy!" Dipping her head, she kissed him spontaneously for the first time.

Their mouths fused. Their tongues dueled. Excitement licked like wildfire through Andrea's veins. A sigh of longing whispered through her lips when he lifted his mouth from hers. Paul responded to the sound of her longing with an answering but restrained sigh.

"I know, my heart, I understand," he murmured. "I feel and share your passion. I want nothing at this moment but to lie in the cradle of your silky thighs, and die there, again and again." He felt her receptive shiver and held her tightly to his hard, aroused body. "But the hour grows late, my Andrea, and we have an important engagement."

Engagement? Andrea frowned. To her admittedly heated senses, there could be nothing more important than having him inside her, filling the aching emptiness. The mere anticipation of their joining set her body on fire.

"Engagement?" she cried. "What engagement?"

"Didn't we arrange separate surprise parties this evening for Celia and Blaine?" he asked, gently nudging her memory into action.

"Oh, my gosh!" Andrea's ardor cooled rapidly with the reminder. "The wedding shower and stag party!"

"Exactly." Paul lowered her slowly to the ground. "The wedding shower and stag party."

Andrea shot a glance at her wrist, then to his eyes. "I forgot my watch! Paul, what time is it?"

Paul laughed. "Time not to panic," he said, reaching for her hand. "The arrangements are all made. All we have to do is get ourselves ready."

After walking back to the campus parking lot, Paul drove Andrea home. As their time was limited, he didn't get out of the car, but did take a moment to kiss her senseless.

"I'll miss you," she moaned when he ended the kiss.

Paul smiled. "I'll be back in less than an hour," he reminded her.

"I know." Andrea pushed her bottom lip out in an exaggerated pout. "I'll still miss you."

Paul kissed her pouting mouth, then pushed her door open. "Go, my heart," he whispered in warning, "before I say the hell with the parties and take you home with me."

Andrea was sorely tempted to pull the door shut again, but reason intruded upon desire. "One hour, Paul," she said as she slid from the seat. "Don't be late."

"I'll be early," he promised, singeing her blood with the smoldering look in his eyes.

"I was beginning to think you weren't going to make it for dinner," Celia observed as Andrea rushed into the house.

"There's plenty of time," Andrea replied in an airy, if breathless, tone. She ran a quick glance over her aunt, then raised an eyebrow. "You're not ready yet," she pointed out, indicating Celia's robe with a flick of her hand.

"All I have to do is toss off this robe and slip into my dress," Celia said. "In case you haven't noticed, I've already fixed my hair and applied my makeup." She grinned. "I've even had a shower for the occasion."

Not like the one you're going to have later this evening, Andrea thought, returning her aunt's grin. Aloud, she grumbled, "Okay, okay, I can hear a hint when it's jabbed at me. I'm on my way." Beginning to feel a tingle of anticipation, she blew a kiss to Celia and headed for her room.

While she showered and dressed, Andrea went over the plans she and Paul had concocted for this evening.

As Blaine's best man, Paul had invited Andrea, Celia, and Blaine out to dinner. The plan was for Paul to leave the door of his home unlocked, and Andrea, after finding a reason to be the last to leave Celia's home, was to leave the cliff house unlocked. Then, while the four of them were at dinner in the restaurant Paul had chosen, which was conveniently located nearby, the friends of Celia and Blaine would gather at the two houses to decorate and prepare for their arrival—Blaine at Paul's home, and Celia at her own house. It was Paul's responsibility to come up with a reasonable excuse to lure Blaine away from Celia.

As she put the finishing touches on her makeup, Andrea smiled. She couldn't wait to hear what reason Paul had devised to get Blaine to go with him to his home.

Everything went off like clockwork. The men arrived on time, Blaine looking handsome in a dark suit and Paul devastating in a white dinner jacket and black slacks.

"Wow!" Blaine exclaimed on sight of his future bride, appearing young and beautiful in an emerald-green, coat-style belted dress.

"Indeed," Paul murmured, his dark blue eyes devouring Andrea, who appeared innocently sensuous in a full-skirted chiffon dress that clung like a caressing hand to her breasts and swirled around her shapely legs when she moved.

Laughing, Celia walked naturally into Blaine's outstretched arms. "I guess that means we've received approval, sugar," she said to Andrea.

"I guess so," Andrea replied, longing to follow her aunt's example, but hesitating uncertainly.

Paul chided her hesitancy with a smile, but simply said, "If everyone's ready, I think we'd better leave."

As arranged, Andrea pretended to have forgotten her purse. "You three go along," she said, turning back. "I'll be with you in a minute." When she left the house seconds later, she was careful to leave the door unlocked.

The restaurant was a favorite of Celia's and Blaine's and had a deserved reputation for its excellent seafood dishes. Andrea, Celia, and Blaine ordered the scampi specialty. Paul chose a large Greek salad with purple olives and chunks of feta cheese. Other than considering his choice of a Greek dish appropriate, Andrea didn't give a second thought to his meatless meal.

The food was delicious and the conversation lively. Andrea thoroughly enjoyed herself, but she did suffer a few anxious moments when they exited the restaurant.

"Oh, darling, will you look at that sky?" Celia said to Blaine. "It seems a shame to waste such a star-studded night by returning to the house."

"Well," Blaine replied, tilting his head back to gaze at the perfect night sky. "We could go somewhere to dance."

With an unconscious display of utter confidence in him, Andrea turned her frantic eyes to Paul. He, in turn, proceeded to prove her confidence well placed.

"That's true," he said to Blaine, momentarily increasing Andrea's anxiety. "But," he continued consideringly, "if we go dancing, we'll be inside and unable to enjoy the night anyway," he pointed out reasonably. "On the other hand, we could return to Celia's house, put on some records or tapes, and dance on the patio under the stars."

"Right," Blaine agreed.

"Wonderful!" Celia exclaimed.

Brilliant, Andrea silently applauded, thinking that

now, even more than before, she couldn't wait to hear what excuse he'd come up with to lure Blaine to his home.

They were almost back to Celia's house before Paul set his machinations in action.

"Oh, by the way, Blaine," Paul said offhandedly. "I have a gift for you and Celia. But, as it's a trifle heavy, I wonder if you'd mind going with me to collect it while Andrea and Celia choose some dance music?"

"Not at all," Blaine replied at once. "But, you know, a gift really wasn't necessary."

"A trifle heavy?" Celia mused aloud. "How intriguing."

Andrea was hard put to contain a burst of laughter. After his stunning display of strength that afternoon, the very idea of him needing help to deliver a wedding gift was not merely funny, it was frankly hilarious.

Andrea was still laughing to herself minutes later as she made a pretense of unlocking the front door. Inside, the house was pitch dark. Pushing the door open, she stood back politely to allow her aunt to enter first.

"I could have sworn I left a lamp turned on," Celia said as she crossed the threshold. Then she exclaimed aloud as the house suddenly blazed with lights.

"Surprise!" called a dozen voices.

The party was an unqualified success. As Celia and Blaine were planning an extended tour to wherever their spirits directed them, Andrea had requested that all gifts be of a personal nature. Not a single guest disappointed her. Amid giggles and more than a few sighs, Celia unwrapped and exclaimed in delight over delicate pieces of sheer lingerie.

When the last of the gifts had been opened and Celia

had tearfully thanked every person with a hug, Andrea glanced at the clock.

If everything was going as planned, she could expect Paul at any minute. The thought was barely completed in Andrea's mind when the front door was flung open. Lugging a large steamer trunk between them, Paul and Blaine entered the room, followed by a dozen men of various ages.

"What in the world!" Celia cried, laughing as she ran to Blaine. "Darling, Andrea and these wonderful women are giving me a bridal shower!"

Dropping his end of the trunk, Blaine swept Celia into his arms. "Do we have great friends, or what?" he demanded, laughing as he swung her around. "These characters actually threw a stag party for me!"

"It was the prof's idea," Mac said over his shoulder, as he crossed the room to Melly.

The rest of the men trailed into the room after Mac.

"Hey!" the head of the history department at Parker exclaimed over the din of laughter and chatter. "Paul promised us some food and liquid refreshments when we got here."

"And I still want to dance on the patio under the stars with my man," Celia announced.

Andrea glanced at Paul and grinned. "Well, prof," she teased. "I think we'd better get to work."

A slow smile tugged at his mouth—and at Andrea's senses—as he released his grip on the trunk and sauntered to her. Taking her hand, he led her into the kitchen, where the women had deposited the food and beverages. The minute they were out of sight of the throng, he drew her into his arms.

"Let's work fast, my Andrea," he whispered against

her mouth. "Because I still want to dance on the patio under the stars with my woman."

And they did dance, long into the star-spangled light. Locked in his embrace, Andrea dreamed of a clearing just beyond a thicket, and the fantastic, and real, man in her arms.

Chapter Nine

By Wednesday of that week, Andrea was beginning to think she'd be unable to find the time to meet Paul in their clearing until after her aunt's wedding, which was to take place on Saturday afternoon.

Celia had found last-minute things for Andrea to do after her classes on both Monday and Tuesday following the parties held Sunday evening.

And so, on Wednesday morning, Andrea went to the breakfast table expecting her aunt to have another list of things for her to do. Resigned to the necessity of giving up her precious time with Paul to help make her aunt's wedding as nearly perfect as possible, Andrea was pleasantly surprised when Celia informed her that there wasn't a thing on the agenda for the day.

"Would you mind being on your own for dinner?" Celia inquired, glancing up from her perusal of the morning paper. "I thought I might run in to San Francisco and do a little shopping." She frowned. "You know, I still haven't found a going-away outfit."

An image of the clothes packed into Celia's walk-in closet swam into Andrea's mind and brought a smile to her lips. Though her aunt had enough outfits to open her own exchange shop, Andrea understood how she was feeling. Celia wanted the perfect ensemble to wear for Blaine.

"I don't mind at all," Andrea replied. "You know, I'm going to be on my own almost every night after you and Blaine leave to go traipsing the world together."

"I know." Celia sighed. "And that's the only part about this that bothers me."

Placing her napkin beside her plate, Andrea rose and circled the table to her aunt. "I thought we had this all settled, Aunt Celia," she said, bending over the older woman to give her a quick hug. "I'll be fine, really. I realize it may be hard for you to accept, considering you have a clear memory of changing my diapers, but I am a big girl now."

Celia's eyes held a sparkle of tears and teasing. "I know," she said. "That's what worries me."

"I can take care of myself," Andrea stated, picking up her books and starting for the door.

"I'd feel a lot better if I knew Paul was taking care of you," Celia called after her.

So would I.

The thought was so startling that Andrea nearly stumbled out of the doorway. Had she come so far in her thinking that she could actually consider letting Paul take care of her? she mused as she drove to the college.

Since Melly wasn't in any of her other classes, Andrea smiled and waved when the pretty blonde rushed up to her as she was entering the lecture hall.

"I need to talk to you, Andrea," Melly said, panting a little from hurrying. "Will you wait for me after class?"

Thinking immediately of Paul, Andrea hesitated a moment. Except for a few rare social occasions, like the shower the previous Sunday, Andrea hadn't seen much of Melly since the beginning of school and her meetings with Paul.

"Of course," Andrea answered after the brief hesitation, positive Paul would understand.

The classroom discussions and arguments were as lively as ever, but Andrea was barely aware of the conversational give-and-take going on around her. Her dreamy-eyed gaze was fastened on the teacher.

His long body propped on the desk behind him, Paul looked relaxed, involved, and utterly fascinating. And he was aware of her fixed stare. At regular intervals, his dark blue eyes would flash to Andrea, drinking her in for an instant before returning to the class at large.

His soft voice washed over her.

". . . but that relates to archaeology, not . . ." he was saying.

". . . I can't wait to hold you, kiss you . . ." she was hearing.

Andrea hadn't grasped a single concept discussed, but she had picked up a lot of exciting vibrations. So bemused was she that she was startled when the students began the usual rustling movements preparatory to leaving the room. Blinking herself out of her daydream, Andrea caught Melly's attention to tell her she'd meet her outside. Then she waited for the hall to empty.

"You have still more errands to run for Celia," Paul said in a soft, patient tone as the door closed behind the last departing student.

"No." Andrea shook her head. "But Melly wants to see me for a minute. Do you mind going on ahead?" She knew it was unnecessary to say where he was to go.

"You'll be there?"

"Yes."

"Then I don't mind." He gave her a smile that sent her flying out of the lecture hall to meet Melly, eager to have their conversation over and gain her freedom to go to him.

Melly was seated on one of the benches scattered around the campus. As Andrea approached her, she noticed that the younger woman looked pale and washed out.

"Melly, is something wrong?" Andrea asked with concern. "You don't look quite right."

Melly shook her head and smiled. "I wanted to tell you I won't be attending classes for a while after this week."

"Something *is* wrong! Melly, what is it?"

"I'm pregnant," Melly blurted out in her usual way.

"Oh, Melly!" Andrea whispered. "What are you going to do?" she asked, more concerned than before.

"Do?" Melly laughed. "I'm going to marry Mac, that's what I'm going to do." She raised her hand to muffle a giggle. "Old sobersides is delighted at the prospect of becoming a father."

Andrea had a flashing image of Mac the previous Sunday, going directly to Melly after arriving at Celia's house. "But, when— I mean . . ." Andrea raised her shoulders in a helpless shrug. "When did you decide all this?"

"Last night," Melly answered. "I received confirmation about the pregnancy yesterday afternoon, and Mac and I made our plans last night." She drew a deep breath before continuing. "We decided to get married immediately, and since I've been afflicted with the most awful morning sickness, I decided to drop out of school for now and pick up again after the semester break in December." She rolled her eyes. "That is, if the morning sickness has passed by then."

Rather dazed by the news, Andrea shook her head, as if trying to clear her mind. "When and where is the wedding to take place?" she finally pulled her wits together enough to ask.

"You did know that I'm from Minnesota?" Melly asked. When Andrea nodded, she went on, "Well, as anxious as I was to get away from home, I now want to go back to be married." She smiled. "I want my family to meet Mac."

"Well, of course you do!" Andrea laughed, clasping Melly's hand. "When will you be leaving?"

Melly grinned. "Not until after your aunt's wedding. I wouldn't miss that for anything!"

Clasping hands, and giggling like teenagers, Andrea and Melly talked for another half-hour. By the time they parted company, Andrea not only knew the date of the wedding but the approximate date the baby was due.

As she hurried through the pine copse, Andrea mused on how very thrilling it must feel to carry and nurture the child of the man you love above all others. She had a dreamy look on her face when she came out of the thicket onto the path.

Paul was waiting for her. Free of the trees, Andrea ran to him.

"Oh, Paul, wait till you hear!" she exclaimed as she ran into his open arms. "Melly's pregnant! She and—"

"I know, my heart," Paul interrupted her gently. "I spoke with Mac about it this morning."

Suddenly worried for her friend, Andrea looked up at Paul in concern. "And how does Mac feel about it . . . the baby, I mean?" she asked, praying Mac had not lied to Melly. She knew everything was all right when Paul smiled.

"I think 'awed' is the most appropriate term."

Andrea sighed in relief and, circling his waist with her arm, turned to walk beside him to the clearing. Thinking of Mac brought a recollection of the past summer and the number of times he had mentioned "the prof" to her. Curious, she glanced sideways at Paul.

"You have a question?" Paul asked softly.

"Umm," Andrea murmured. "I was wondering how I missed meeting you all summer. I recall Aunt Celia mentioning that you had just returned that night you came with Blaine to the house. Were you on vacation?"

"Yes," he replied. "I was visiting my parents."

"In Texas?" Andrea glanced at him.

Paul shook his head. "No. My parents no longer live in Texas. They returned to my father's homeland several years ago."

"Oh." Andrea was quiet for a moment, lost in visions of the blue waters of the Aegean Sea and the dazzling, sun-splashed Acropolis. The vision faded when they came to the clearing. "No wonder your skin is so bronzed," she murmured.

Paul laughed. "Yes, my father's homeland is bathed in sunlight." He eyed the gnarled trunk of the tree and then, laughing again, dropped easily to the ground.

Sitting down beside him, Andrea went into his arms. "You're parents are both scientists, aren't they?" she asked, snuggling close to his lean body.

"My mother is a biologist," he answered, rubbing his cheek against her hair. "My father is a . . . naturalist."

Andrea didn't notice his brief pause. She was too busy noticing the shivers running rampant from her head to her toes. Loving the sensation, she held him closer.

"Are you cold?" Paul drew his head back to look at her. "We are close to the warmth of my home, Andrea."

Andrea suddenly did feel cold—a quivery cold—inside her. For reasons she couldn't name, she felt hesitant about going with him to his house. "No!" She cleared her throat, then said more calmly, "No, Paul, I'm not cold at all."

Paul exhaled a sigh. "You're not quite ready yet, are you, my Andrea?"

Andrea had a strange feeling that he was referring to much more than her not being ready to enter his home. Pushing the notion away, she answered, "No, not yet, Paul. Please be patient with me a little longer."

"As long as I can be, my heart," he murmured, confusing her even more. "You'll like my house," he went on. Then, after a moment's hesitation, he added, "It's an exact replica of the house that's waiting for me in my father's homeland."

Andrea jolted back in surprise. "Waiting for you?" she repeated, staring at him. "I don't understand. Are you saying that you are planning to move there someday?"

"Yes," he answered. "It's where I feel most at home."

Trying to deny the feeling of desertion seeping through her, Andrea cried, "But what about your work? Your career?"

Paul drew her against him again. "I can work there, my heart," he assured her. "I can love there, also."

Love. It was the first time the word had been mentioned between them. That word and others joined the feelings seeping through her.

Love.

Trust.

Betrayal.

Suddenly frightened and not even sure why, Andrea clung to the reassuring strength of his body. "Hold me, Paul," she pleaded. "Hold me."

"I intend to, my Andrea," he said. Tilting her head back with his hand, Paul lowered his mouth to hers. "I intend to hold you, and never let you go."

With the touch of his mouth to hers, the inexplicable fear inside Andrea turned into understandable passion. Feeling a deeper hunger for him than she would have believed herself capable of feeling for any man—any *physical* man—Andrea curled her arms around his neck and returned his kiss with abandon.

His mouth as hungry as hers, if not hungrier, Paul deepened the kiss, tasting her sweetness with his lips and his probing tongue. His hands moved over her back, sending cascading thrills through her when his fingers brushed the outer curves of her breasts.

Receptive to the feelings and needs deep inside her that only he possessed the power to arouse, Andrea responded with an equal heat to his kiss and matched the caressing movements of his hands with her own.

"Andrea, Andrea." Repeating her name in an aching whisper, Paul slowly lowered her to the bed of grass and covered her trembling body with his own.

Instinctively, Andrea parted her thighs, making a cradle for his body. Pushing himself back, away from her, Paul stared into her eyes, then carefully slid her skirt up, revealing her legs. The tremors inside Andrea intensified to a quake as he settled his taut body in the valley of her silken thighs.

The rough denim of his jeans brushed, then pressed against the soft silk of her panties, creating a sensuous friction that shot sparks of fire into the depths of her passion, causing her to cry out in unexpected pleasure.

"Paul!"

In response to her cry, Paul moved his body forward in a restrained thrust, making her fully aware of the extent of his arousal, feeding her own expanding excitement.

Instantly obeying an inner command from her senses, Andrea grasped his hips and pulled him more tightly against her, while simultaneously arching her hips into the denim-constrained fullness of his body. The results of her actions were both inflaming and frustrating. Needing to feel him, touch him, she released her grip on his hips and moved her hands up his body to the buttons on his shirt.

As if Paul had once again read her mind, he pushed himself back and away from her. Chilled by his withdrawal, Andrea gazed up at him in confusion.

"Paul . . . I want—"

"Yes, my heart," he whispered over her gasping voice. "I want . . . too." Grasping her gently by the shoulders, he drew her up with him. When she was seated in front of him, he lifted her hands and returned them to his shirt buttons.

Andrea stared at him a long moment, hesitant to begin what had years ago always been an awkward, embarrassing exercise. Chilling memories stormed through her, challenging the strength of her desire for Paul. Caught between the then and the now, she gazed at him, her hazel eyes beseeching his help.

Paul smiled and raised his hands to her shirt, transforming her hesitancy into immediate willingness. With his guidance, Andrea discovered the erotic thrill that could be derived from slowly, sensuously undressing a man while he lovingly undressed her.

After each piece of clothing was discarded, they devoted infinite time to the tactile exploration of the exposed area of each other's bodies. There was no groping or clutching or grabbing, only exquisite, senses-stirring caresses. And with each successive caress, each new sensation, Andrea's body became more alive, more vibrant, and more deeply attuned to her own needs and to Paul's desires. Her senses fully awakened for the first time in her life, Andrea shivered in anticipation as Paul again carefully lowered her to the bed of grass. This time when he moved into the cradle of her thighs, there was no barrier between them, material or spiritual.

"Now, my Andrea, we are truly free to express all our feelings," Paul whispered, arching his body against hers in a teasing thrust.

"Yes!" Andrea cried out in a raspy whisper. "Oh, Paul, yes . . . yes!" As before, her hands slid to his hips to urge him into the ultimate caress.

Paul moved against her once more, inciting her passion. Fire leaped from one nerve end to another throughout Andrea's body, then gathered to form a blaze in the deepest part of her femininity.

Murmuring softly, incoherently, Andrea flexed her fingers, sinking her nails into his flesh in a silent plea for his possession.

Paul responded immediately. Leaning over her, he covered her open mouth with his and then, simultaneously, thrust his tongue into her mouth and his body into hers.

Tension. Tension as she had only dreamed it spiraled through Andrea. But now, in reality, the coiled ribbon of tension was even tighter. Clinging to him, sobbing his name into his mouth, Andrea pursued the tension on its flaming upward spiral to the gates of paradise. When the gates flew open, the coil of tension snapped, flinging Andrea into a universe blazing with brilliant, pulsating lights.

"Paul!" Andrea cried his name.

Her own name echoed back to her in his hoarse cry of release.

"Andrea!"

Their shuddering bodies locked together in the most intimate embrace known to lovers, they descended from the realm of paradise into the aftermath of utter completion.

Ecstasy.

To Andrea, "ecstasy" had always been a word without meaning, a word she had, moreover, strongly suspected had no actual meaning. Now, with Paul at rest but still vibrant and alive inside her, Andrea's tingling body defined the word "ecstasy" for her.

Intuitively seeking to enhance the definition, Andrea smoothed her palms over Paul's body, the instrument of her delightful edification. He stirred, murmured, and responded to her exploration of his body by pressing his open mouth over the crest of one of her breasts.

Inspired by the electrical thrill she experienced from his reaction to her caress, Andrea reciprocated by tasting his love-moistened shoulder with the tip of her tongue. This time his stirring movement came from within her body, while Paul, in turn, drew the crest of her breast into his mouth and suckled delicately.

Love play.

The phrase was yet another Andrea had believed existed only in the minds of dreamers and wishful thinkers. Yet now, having had that phrase also defined in reality, Andrea became an avid seeker of truth.

At times murmuring inciting love words, at others laughing together, Andrea and Paul took turns giving pleasure to each other.

While buried deep inside her, Paul supported his body on one forearm and examined her form with his free hand. Beginning at her forehead, he outlined her features with his fingers. He minutely inspected every bone and hollow of her throat before his hand moved lower. He doubled the intensity of his attention by caressing her breasts with both his hand and his mouth. Andrea was barely breathing by the time he slid his hand down the sloping incline of her midsection to her flat belly, and she gasped a quick breath when his fingers ascended the mound of her desire to gently probe the area where their respective bodies were fused into one.

In her turn, Andrea stroked every inch of Paul's body she could reach. Like him, she began with his perfect features, marveling anew at his masculine beauty. From his face she slid her hands to his neck, then measured the width of his shoulders. As he had, she gave particular attention to his chest, returning to him the thrill he'd given her by suckling on his flat male nipples while tangling her fingers in the silky whorls of black hair on his chest. His breathing grew rough and shallow as she slid her palms down his torso, and he arched his back to give her access to the lower half of his body. In comparison to the thick black mane on his head and the curls on his chest, which tapered in a thin line to his loins, the rest of his body was completely smooth and free of hair.

Fascinated with her discovery, Andrea stroked his flanks and thighs. His skin was taut but pliant and as sleek and gleaming as warm satin. As she stroked him, Andrea had a fleeting image of a dolphin leaping from the water, its skin sleek and smooth and shimmering in the sunlight.

The vision was intriguing and Andrea might have pursued it, but at that instant she felt Paul's life force leap inside her. Her half-closed eyes flew open and she gave a little cry of surprise.

"Yes, my Andrea," he said in that soft tone that sent shivers tumbling through her. "The pathway to paradise beckons once more." Lowering his head, he whispered against her parted lips, "Will you ride the pathway with me?"

In answer, Andrea curled her arms around his neck and her legs around his hips and arched her body into the increasing tempo of his movements.

Once again the ribbon of tension unfurled inside Andrea until, soaring free, her rejoicing spirit attained the beauty of pure ecstasy. But this time when she cried aloud it was not to utter his name but to speak an inner accepted truth.

"I love you! I love you!"

And this time the echo that returned to her was not the sound of her own name but the hoarse sound of Paul's voice repeating the binding declaration.

"As I have always loved you."

Always? The word flashed through Andrea's mind, then was gone, erased by the intensity of the sensations pulsating through her entire being.

Exhausted, replete, Andrea surrendered to the warmth of Paul's body protecting hers. She fell asleep stroking the satin-smooth skin beneath the hair on his chest.

"Andrea." The soft sound of Paul's voice drew her from the depths of dreamless slumber. "Wake up, my love. It's getting late, and Celia might be worried."

My love.

Into Andrea's sleep-fuzzy mind came a memory of a dream and of her imaginary lover whispering that he was her love, as she was his love, had always been his love, from the moment of her creation. But she had created him! Andrea thought in hazy confusion, struggling to shake off the clinging tendrils of sleep. And he had left her dreams to merge his essence with that of his physical duplicate. And her love had loved her, had made passionate, exquisite love to her, in her dreams and in her physical reality!

Were they one and the same man?

The inner voice of renewed doubt drove the last cobwebs of sleep from her mind. She needed to be awake, had to be awake to prove that he was real. Andrea opened her eyes and gave a heartfelt sigh of relief.

Appearing very real and wholly physical, Paul was smiling at her. "You sleep deeply after you release your concealed inhibitions, my Andrea," he murmured. "It's growing dark and the evening breeze carries a chill."

Until he mentioned it, Andrea hadn't noticed. In addition to giving her the protective warmth of his body, Paul had covered her with his shirt.

"I'm not cold," she said, raising her eyes to his. "But you must be. You're completely exposed to the wind."

Paul shook his head. "No. I seldom mind the cold. But it is getting late. Celia will be concerned." He smiled and then reminded her of their vigorous exercise. "And you must be starving."

"Aunt Celia won't be worried, because she's not home," she said, raising her arms over her head and stretching luxuriously. "But you're right. I am starving."

Paul's eyes darkened, and as if he couldn't resist the lure of her body, stretched out so invitingly close to him, he drew his hand slowly down the entire length of her form.

Andrea shivered receptively and whispered his name.

Paul proved himself the stronger of the two of them. With a last lingering look at her, he put her away from him and stood up. Then, bending over her, he lifted her high in his arms for one last kiss before releasing her to reach for his clothing.

Later, sitting close to each other in a corner booth of a fast food restaurant, laughing and murmuring, they devoured a large pizza and two side orders of salad for dinner.

It was late when Paul drove Andrea home. As they neared the house, Andrea sighed. "I won't be able to be with you until Saturday. I have to work tomorrow and Friday."

"I know." Paul sighed, too. "And tomorrow night you have to attend Celia's lady-bachelor party. And Friday night I have to go to Blaine's bachelor party."

"And then the wedding on Saturday," Andrea said.

"Yes." Paul slanted a blatantly sexy smile at her. "We can slow-dance at the reception."

He reluctantly left her at the door after a long, deep good-night kiss. Hugging the memory of his thrilling kisses and even more thrilling lovemaking, Andrea showered, slipped on a nightshirt, and fell into bed. Refusing to think of the possible consequences of her actions, she drifted off to sleep with a tiny smile of satisfaction on her love-softened mouth.

The wedding was solemn and beautiful.

Standing beside her aunt, listening to Celia exchange vows of marriage with Blaine, Andrea recalled another wedding the previous spring. Mingled with the voices of Celia and Blaine were the memory voices of her friend Alycia and her bridegroom, Sean, and she felt a sudden yearning to see them and Karla.

The yearning persisted throughout the brief ceremony, but dissolved when she encountered the warmth in Paul's eyes as she glanced at him after it was over.

Andrea did slow-dance with Paul during the wedding reception. And she fast-danced with Mac and did the tango with Blaine. Flushed and laughing, she visited the buffet table with Paul and pondered the wide and varied selections offered. In the end, she passed up the meats for a combination of seafood. While they were eating, Andrea noticed that Paul had passed up both the meats and the seafood.

Frowning, Andrea rifled through her memory images of every meal she'd shared with him. As far as she could remember, she had never seen Paul eat meat, poultry, or seafood.

Taking note of her frown, Paul raised his eyebrows. "Is there something wrong with your meal?" he asked.

"No." Andrea shook her head. "I was wondering about your meal." She glanced at the assortment of vegetables and pasta salad on his plate.

Paul followed her glance with his eyes. Then he, too, frowned. "What were you wondering about?"

Andrea sighed. "I guess I was wondering if you are

one of those California vegetarian health-food nuts I've heard so much about."

His lips twitching, Paul slowly shook his head. "No, Andrea," he replied, laughter threatening on his voice. "I assure you I am not a California vegetarian health-food nut."

"Do you eat meat or fowl or fish?" she asked.

"No."

"Why?"

"Because, my Andrea," Paul answered softly, "in my father's homeland, we do not eat flesh."

Chapter Ten

ANDREA PUZZLED OVER PAUL'S calmly stated reason for not eating flesh during the remainder of the reception. While dancing, talking, and just generally being sociable, she examined his claim, looking for hidden meanings in it. Perhaps, if she could have accepted his words at face value, she might have been able to shrug off his assertion.

But as Andrea was swiftly coming to the realization that everything Paul said could be taken as literal fact— regardless how incomprehensible those facts were to her—she couldn't just accept it at face value. Yet any other explanation didn't make sense. She knew that the people of Greece *did* eat meat, fowl, and fish.

Andrea considered asking him to elaborate on his statement, but rejected the idea, simply because she felt intuitively that she wouldn't particularly like his explanation. In the end, she decided to forget the whole thing . . . which she had been doing a lot lately, in relation to Paul.

By Sunday morning, Andrea had dismissed her disturbing discussion with Paul from her mind. She was already missing her aunt, and Celia had only been away from the house one night.

But Celia was back at the house again by midmorning on Sunday, checking to make certain she hadn't overlooked anything. Over coffee, she went through her itinerary with Andrea . . . for at least the fifth time.

The plan was for Celia and Blaine to fly to New York that evening. After a few days of sight-seeing, they would fly on to London for more sight-seeing. From London, the couple would cross the English Channel to France. After a week in Paris, they were booked on a cruise liner bound for the Mediterranean.

Since the farthest she had ever traveled was her flight from Pennsylvania to California, Andrea thought Celia and Blaine's plans sounded exciting.

But the flurry of activity and excitement was over, leaving Andrea feeling deflated and let down after she and Paul waved the couple on their way at the airport.

"You're very quiet," Paul observed after a nearly silent drive back to the house. "Are you tired?"

"Yes." Andrea sighed, then laughed at herself. "I suppose I'm feeling a little let down now that all the excitement is over."

"Ah, but, my Andrea," Paul said softly as he pulled the car into the driveway, "*is* the excitement over?"

That night and every night for the next two weeks, they made glorious love, not on a bed of grass, but in Andrea's bed of brass.

A week after the wedding, Andrea received an invitation to the opening of her friend Karla's art gallery in

Sedona, Arizona. Memories assailed her as she read the note Karla had written on the bottom of the embossed card.

"Dear Andrea," Karla wrote. "Do you miss Alycia and me as much as I miss you and Alycia?" She then went on in her practical way: "Although I know you probably won't be able to make it to my grand opening, I'll be thinking of you and wishing you could share it with me."

Tears misted Andrea's eyes as she scanned the note a second time, and she was swamped by a longing to see her friends. On the spot Andrea decided that she *would* make it to Karla's opening, even if she had to scrape the bottom of her bank account to pay the air fare.

The following Saturday afternoon, Andrea was staring out the window at the dreary rain-spattered day when the phone rang. The day brightened when she heard the voice of her caller.

"Alycia! Where are you? How are you? How is Sean?" she asked in a rush.

"Andrea, it's so good to hear your voice." Alycia laughed. "I'm in New York. Sean and I are both fine." She hesitated a moment, then went on, "And I'm calling to tell you that, whether you had planned to or not, you're going to be at Karla's opening next week."

"I am?" Andrea laughed. "Well, as a matter of fact I am! I mean, I was planning to be there."

"Have you made your flight arrangements yet?" Alycia asked.

"No," Andrea said. "I was going to do that on Monday."

"Well, don't," Alycia ordered. "Sean will take care of everything from here."

"Why?"

"Oh, didn't you know?" Alycia asked seriously. "Sean has a great travel agent. He books us into Florida in August and Alaska in January!"

Andrea laughed . . . with tears in her eyes. It was so wonderful to hear Alycia's banter again. "If you get really lucky, that agent might be able to book you onto the first flight to a friendly planet," Andrea responded.

"Naw," Alycia came back. "This guy doesn't know any friendly people, never mind friendly aliens."

"Too bad," Andrea sympathized. "It might be fun, and it couldn't be dull."

"Yeah, well, I'll stick to the earth, thank you," Alycia retorted. "You're the space nut."

"Was," Andrea said on a sigh.

"Hey, Andrea, there's time," Alycia chided gently. "Don't give up hope on NASA."

"I kinda have," Andrea told her. "I'm back in school, doing my postgraduate thing. What have you been up to?"

"Doing my history thing," Alycia said. "I'm helping Sean research his latest tome."

"You sound happy," Andrea said softly.

"I am happy," Alycia replied. "But I miss my former partners in idiocy sometimes."

"So do I," Andrea admitted.

"So, we'll be together next week," Alycia said. "Don't buy a ticket, but do expect to hear from the airline confirming your flight. Sean will take care of everything. Okay?"

Her eyes misting with memories of Sean taking care of several dinners at the apartment she and Karla and Alycia had shared, Andrea surrendered and answered, "Okay."

Andrea continued to hold the receiver in her hand for

a few seconds after saying a reluctant good-bye to her friend—as if, by not cradling the receiver she could maintain the connection to Alycia just a little longer. Her smile was rueful as she returned to stand at the living room window after finally replacing the receiver.

The window faced southwest, affording a panoramic view of the coastline and the Pacific Ocean. Andrea didn't see the view, or the rain, or the dark clouds hanging over the ocean for, though she was staring out through the window, she was looking inward, at her self.

The view inside was every bit as murky as the scene beyond the window. Like the day, which was heavy with atmospheric pressure, Andrea felt weighted with the pressure of sadness and doubt . . . a lot of doubt.

She was alone. Again.

Feeling the emptiness of the house and of her life closing in around her, Andrea sighed and pressed her forehead to the cool windowpane.

Although she saw Paul every weekday in class, had dinner with him most evenings, and slept with him every night, Andrea knew that she was basically alone.

Her aloneness was by no means new or unusual. It was like a familiar but undesirable companion. That companion had moved in with her at a very early age, and while she stood helplessly by as others she loved left her, the unwanted companion remained.

Although Andrea, as a child, had given her love openly and joyfully, she had grown more restrained as each loved one deserted her. Her father had been the first to leave her, and though he'd had no choice about leaving, Andrea, being very young, had felt that he left because of some fault in her. Her mother had been the next in line, deserting Andrea for the love of a man.

Then Zach had left her for another woman, and it was after Zach's desertion that Andrea began to close in on herself.

And there were others, not actually deserters, but followers of their own dreams and pursuits. Alycia, Karla, Celia, and even Melly were all now, in effect, gone from Andrea's life.

Andrea was alone. Again.

And she was in love with Paul.

Ever since she had cried the words of love to him that Sunday afternoon in the clearing, Andrea had repeatedly asked herself if her declaration had been a spontaneous response to the shattering experience she had shared with him or if, in fact, she was in love with him. After hours of examining her feelings, emotions, and rational mind, she had reached the conclusion that she did love Paul, that she was in love with him.

In truth, Andrea loved almost everything about Paul. She loved his incredible male beauty, she loved the mysterious depth of his blue eyes, she loved his soft voice and tender smile, she loved his compassion and tolerance, his inner strength and his outward understanding. She even loved the ways in which he was different from other men. But most of all, she loved talking with him, laughing with him, making love with him.

Oh, yes, Andrea thought, brushing a film of moisture from her eyes. She did indeed love Paul. But Andrea found no joy in the acknowledgment.

Within Andrea's only frame of reference, she equated the word "love" with disillusionment, pain, and eventual, inevitable betrayal. And she knew, had learned the painful way, that it was infinitely safer not to give her love, but instead to hide it away within the confines of her aloneness.

The unmistakable purr of Paul's fantastic car pulling into the driveway drew Andrea out of her inner, secret hiding place.

How strange, she mused, turning away from the window and donning a smile for her lover. How strange that she, who had looked forward with such eagerness and high hopes to the possibility of future space travel, had so few hopes for her own future.

"You're withdrawing inside yourself again, my Andrea." Paul made the observation the instant he saw her face . . . or her eyes. "You are deliberately distancing yourself from me . . . from us."

Andrea forced a laugh . . . It sounded forced. Compensating, she shrugged. "I was just thinking."

"About what?" he asked, crossing the room to her.

"Alycia called a little while ago. She and Sean are going to Karla's grand opening." Andrea didn't need to explain further; she had told Paul all about her friends during their weeks of getting to know each other.

"Then why are you sad?" Paul asked, tapping in as usual to her emotional state.

"I'm not sad," Andrea lied. "I'm just . . . contemplative."

The expression in his eyes told her he knew she was lying to him. His sigh, followed by the gentle smile that curved his mouth, told her he would not challenge her . . . at least not for the moment.

Paul was especially gentle with her during the days remaining before Andrea was to leave for Arizona, and he was especially passionate during the nights.

"Shall we walk awhile?" he asked after class the day before she was to leave.

Andrea answered silently by slipping her hand into his and falling into step with his long, easy stride. She wasn't surprised when he headed for the copse of pine trees. Though he would spend the night in her bed and drive her to the airport in the morning, inside her mind, there but unformed, Andrea knew he was taking her to their special place, where they could say good-bye in private.

The early November afternoon was mild. A crisp breeze carried the scent of fall, stirring memories in Andrea of the beautiful autumns in her home in Pennsylvania.

A feeling of melancholy settled over Andrea, and when they arrived at the clearing, a sad smile curved her lips as she looked around her. Over a year had passed since she had first seen the clearing in her dreams. Now it seemed to have happened long ago, and to another person.

"Come, my heart," Paul said softly. "It's time to go home."

Her shoulders drooping with dejection, Andrea moved automatically when Paul tugged on her hand. But instead of turning back toward the campus, he followed the path away from the clearing.

Uneasiness began to unfurl inside Andrea. She raised her head and glanced around with narrowed, alert eyes. "Where are we going?" she asked, knowing the answer.

"Home," Paul replied simply.

Inside her mind, Andrea was envisioning a dream in which she had walked along this same path. In the dream she'd felt happy, content. But this was not a dream, she reminded herself. And she was not feeling happy . . . She was feeling frightened and reluctant to go on. The beginnings of panic crawled up her nerves toward her throat as she and Paul drew near a bend in the path. The scent of the sea was pervasive. A seabird sounded its mournful cry. Her dream thoughts spun out of control in her mind.

She was almost there.

She was almost home.

Everything that had happened to her, every unusual incident, pulsed in brilliant flashes through her memory.

The first time she had seen Paul through the window of the coffee shop.

Her dream lover telling her that she had nothing to fear from Paul Hellka.

The incredible experience she'd had with Paul on the beach before discovering that he swam with sharks.

Paul's uncanny ability to read her mind.

Paul telling her that in his father's homeland they did not eat flesh.

Paul's display of strength that appeared to be beyond human possibility.

Melly's observation: *Maybe the man's not human.*

"No!" Andrea cried aloud, coming to a dead stop on the bend in the path.

"Andrea." Paul's soft voice held no censure, no reproof, only an unspoken plea for her trust.

All the confusion and fear she had pushed to the farthest reaches of her mind came storming back into her consciousness. And in exactly the same way she had done on the day he first took her to the clearing, Andrea stared at him and cried out the same questions . . . only this time she changed one word of the second query.

"Who are you? *What* are you?"

"I am your love," Paul answered. "For always and forever. I have been since the day you were created."

Too much. Too much. Andrea had reached the outermost boundaries of believability. Unable and unwilling to accept what he was telling her, she reacted exactly as she had in her last dream with her love. She pulled her hand free of his and ran away from him, ignoring his cry.

"Andrea! Come home!"

The drone of the jet engines lulled Andrea into a half-sleep. She was bone-tired, but her mind refused to let her rest. She was on her way home, or at any rate, back to California and her aunt's house on the cliffs.

Pretending to be the Andrea her friends knew had just about depleted Andrea's reserves. A faint smile shadowed her vulnerable lips for a moment as she recalled the reunion she had celebrated with Alycia, Sean, and Karla. The reunion had been doubly satisfying for them all, as the grand opening of Karla's gallery had been a smashing success.

In addition, Andrea strongly suspected that there was, or soon would be, a man in Karla's life. For, despite Karla's insistence that she felt nothing for the man, there had been a new brightness to her eyes when she spoke of the imposing, ruggedly handsome world-famous painter, Jared Cradowg.

Andrea felt genuinely happy that the future seemed to be opening up in exciting ways for her friends. But in relation to her own future, Andrea could see nothing but a continuation of her state of aloneness.

Although it had been only a few short days since she had run away from Paul, Andrea missed him to a degree of intensity she would not previously have believed possible. The memory of him, the need for him, was like a constantly twisting knife in her heart. The pain was unbearable.

Paul was not at the airport to meet her, as they had arranged for him to be less than a week ago. But then, although she had harbored a secret hope that he'd come, Andrea really hadn't expected him to show up.

She had not seen or heard from him since that afternoon . . . was it really only three days ago? Without knowing how she knew—feelings? intuitions?—Andrea was certain that he was waiting for her to sort herself out, resolve her inner conflicts, and work up her courage to go to him, to where he was waiting for her, in his house beyond the path, the house he referred to as *her* home.

She was alone. Again.

During the weeks that followed Andrea's return from Arizona she was entirely alone. She did not return to school. She saw no one except on two or three occasions when she was forced to shop for groceries. Cloistered inside the area around the cliff house, Andrea paced the rooms or walked the little crescent beach, waging an inner battle with her crippling fears—of betrayal, of committing her love and herself, and of the eerie differences that set Paul apart from other men.

Thanksgiving came and went, unnoticed by Andrea. The weather was damp and raw, but except for putting on a jacket when she left the house to prowl the beach, Andrea didn't notice that, either. The pain of missing Paul had not lessened; it had deepened.

In the first week of December, Andrea received a phone call from Karla, happily demanding, not requesting, that Andrea return to Arizona at the end of that week to stand witness, along with Alycia, at her marriage to Jared Cradowg. Laughing and crying with her friend, Andrea promised to be there.

Though her inner battle had raged on during her

weeks of solitude, Andrea knew that the force of her love for Paul had sent her fear into retreat. Strangely, the call from Karla was instrumental in routing the fear completely and forever.

For wasn't Karla the practical, earthbound member of their unlikely trio? Andrea reminded herself. And hadn't it always been Karla who had held out at all costs against the concept of loving a man to the point of total commitment? And if the practical, earthbound Karla was no longer afraid to let her spirit soar on the wings of love, Andrea asked herself, why should she, the believer in space travel, be afraid to let her love take flight? The answer came from deep within Andrea.

She was no longer alone.

Dusk was creeping over the earth as Andrea approached the bend in the path. She was calm, happy, and at peace with herself at last. She smiled as a seabird cried overhead. It was fitting for the occasion.

She was almost there.

She was almost home.

Without a twinge of fear or a second thought, Andrea followed the bend and continued along the path. A gasp of delighted surprise whispered through her lips when she sighted the house. Seemingly carved out of the cliff face, the rock and glass structure, like the man himself, possessed a natural breathtaking beauty.

Paul was waiting for her in the open doorway.

Without a twinge of fear, or a second thought, Andrea ran the last few steps and into his arms.

"Welcome home, my heart," Paul said in his achingly familiar soft voice. "I've missed you."

"I love you. I love you." Andrea murmured the words, as he swept her into his arms and carried her through the house to his bedroom.

"And I love you, my Andrea," Paul said. "I have always loved you."

"I love you," she whispered, as he slowly removed her clothes and helped her to remove his.

"I love you," his voice echoed hers, as he crushed her mouth to his and gently lowered her to the bed.

"Oh, Paul, I love you!" Andrea cried moments later, as once again she was blinded by the brilliance of paradise.

"My Andrea! My Andrea!" his hoarse cry rang sweetly in her ears. "I love you!"

It was fully dark outside when Andrea woke from a lovely dream in which she and Paul had walked hand in hand, ecstatic together, in a strange and unfamiliar but fantastically beautiful land. So stunningly beautiful had the land been—warm and sunlit, the earth verdant and filled with an abundance of colorful life, a true paradise —that for a moment Andrea mourned the passing of the dream. Then she turned her head and the memory faded, overshadowed by the beauty of the man standing by a wall of glass, smiling for her . . . only for her.

"You smiled in your sleep, my heart," Paul said softly.

"I had a beautiful dream," Andrea murmured.

In the dim indirect lighting, his eyes seemed to glow with inner amusement. "Dreams do come true, you know," he whispered. "I had a dream of you . . . and here you are."

"Yes," Andrea replied. "Here I am. And I haven't really seen the 'here' where I am." Unconcerned and unembarrassed by her nudity, she pushed the bedcovers back and left the bed.

Scooping a silky robe from the back of a chair, Paul

held it out for her. Andrea felt a sensuous thrill as the silky material glided over her skin. Knowing the robe belonged to Paul, she wrapped it tightly around herself. The smile that curved his sculpted mouth and darkened his eyes told her that he knew what she was feeling.

Curious about his house, Andrea glanced around the room. Her eyes halted at a large, open flight bag on a low chest against the wall. Slowly, Andrea raised her puzzled eyes to his.

"I have received word from my father," Paul said in answer to her silent question. "I must return to my homeland."

Stunned, Andrea stared at him in mute appeal.

"Come with me, my heart." Raising his arm, Paul held his hand, palm up, out to her. "Love me as I love you. Come with me. Trust me."

Andrea hesitated for an instant. She didn't know where he might take her. She didn't know if he was asking her to go with him to Greece or . . . Andrea didn't know . . . And in truth, she didn't care. She would be with her love. Her instant of hesitation was over.

Smiling into his eyes, Andrea placed her hand in his with utter and complete trust.

Epilogue

THE DECOR OF THE restaurant was underplayed elegance. Black-jacketed waiters and waitresses moved with silent efficiency among tables occupied by well-dressed patrons. Conversation was relaxed, low-key.

At a round table before a wide undraped window, a dark-suited russet-haired man raised a long-stemmed glass in salute to the couple seated opposite him and then to the woman seated next to him.

"To your health and happiness and to long years of artistic production together," Sean Halloran toasted the pair.

"Hear, hear!" Alycia Halloran said, raising her glass to her lips.

Jared Cradowg and his bride of two hours, the former Karla Janowitz, smiled into each other's eyes as they sipped their wine in acceptance of the toast.

"Thank you, Sean," Jared said, tilting his glass at the

other couple. "And to your continued happiness."

"It was a lovely wedding," Alycia murmured, smiling mistily at Karla.

"Yes." Karla nodded. "Only one thing kept it from being absolutely perfect."

"Andrea," Alycia said, sighing.

"Why isn't she here?" Karla exclaimed softly, recalling Andrea's promise to stand beside her.

"Where is she?" Alycia cried in concern, recalling the endless ringing of the phone in California when she had tried to reach her friend.

The men spoke simultaneously.

"Darling, try not to worry—" Sean began.

"Karla, honey, I'm sure she's all—" Jared began.

They were interrupted by the arrival of the wine steward, who came to a halt with a flourish at their table. Before their amazed eyes, the officious-looking man whipped the excellent bottle of domestic champagne they had ordered out of the standing ice bucket and waved imperiously to the waiter at his heels in a silent command to remove their glasses.

"Now, wait a minute—" Jared began.

"What's this all—" Sean began.

"Ladies, gentlemen," the wine steward interrupted, nodding to the waiter, who immediately set clean glasses in front of the puzzled foursome. "I was ordered to deliver this wine to you." With a superior expression, he held a well-known, very expensive bottle of imported champagne aloft for their inspection.

Frowning in confusion, the foursome stared at the bottle and then at one another as the steward poured the bubbling liquid into their glasses. When each glass was half full, he placed the bottle in the bucket and held out a white envelope. "I was asked to give you this with the wine." Turning smartly, he walked away.

Since Sean had been seated closest to the steward, he had handed the envelope to him. Raising his russet brows, Sean looked at his companions.

"You might as well see what this is all about," Jared drawled.

"Right," Sean agreed and tore the envelope open. He withdrew a single folded sheet of paper. Flipping it open, he read the contents aloud. "'Dear friends,'" Sean began in a brisk, businesslike tone. "'Please accept this bottle of champagne in celebration. I am sorry if I have disappointed you today.'" Sean's tone and voice softened as he went on. "'Karla and Jared, I wish you all the love and happiness that I know Alycia and Sean share. Though I can't be there with you in person, please know that I am thinking about you and that I love all of you.'"

"Andrea," Alycia whispered when Sean paused to glance up at them.

"But where is she?" Karla cried, clasping Jared's hand for support.

Sean returned his attention to the note, found the place where he had left off, then continued reading, "'I know that you are probably concerned about me, but please don't be. For, you see, I am also celebrating this night. I am with the man I love. His name is Paul . . . and he is everything. Be as happy for me as I am for the four of you.'" Sean glanced up as he finished, "'All Paul's and my love, Andrea.'"

There was silence around the table for several seconds. Tears ran unchecked down the faces of the women and glittered in the eyes of the men.

Then Alycia slowly raised her glass. "To Andrea and

her Paul," said the woman who believed in yesterday. "May they love each other always."

Karla held her glass with trembling fingers. "To Andrea and Paul," repeated the woman who was firmly entrenched in today, "for all their tomorrows, wherever they may be."

The meeting of four glasses over the table was reflected in the wide window. Beyond the brightly lit window, the chill, crisp air of late autumn afforded a spectacular view of a midnight-dark sky ablaze with brilliant sparkling stars.

A man and woman stood arm in arm at the rail of the luxury cruise ship, gazing at the panorama of a night sky glittering with millions of stars. The woman was weeping softly, not from sadness but with joy. In her hand she held a small piece of white paper. The message written on it was brief: "Dear Aunt Celia and Uncle Blaine, I love you. I am happy. Paul is taking care of me. Andrea."

SECOND CHANCE AT LOVE

COMING NEXT MONTH

OVERNIGHT SENSATION #460
by Dianne Thomas
A fate arranged by her Great-Aunt
Mercedes, Jessie finds herself in the
constant company of TV idol Cam Holder,
whose charm and good looks have
her forgetting the very reason
they were brought together...

THE SILENT HEART #461
by Kelly Adams
Laura Kincaid is more than
striking—she is poetic, expressive, and
hearing-impaired. Senatorial
candidate David Evers surrenders his
heart to her eloquence and fire. But her
deafness has interfered before, and she's
determined not to be hurt again...

SECOND CHANCE AT LOVE

BE SURE TO READ...

FOUL PLAY #456
by Steffie Hall
Handsome veterinarian Jake Elliott
has already rescued Amy Klasse once; now
her reputation's at stake. Will Jake
be able to save it—and their
newfound love, too?

THE RIALTO AFFAIR #457
by Jan Mathews
Two years ago, Dr. Amanda Pearson
gave criminal lawyer Tyler Marshall more
than the professional testimony he needed to
win his case. Amanda had given herself,
too. Now Ty's back—and he won't
let her defense rest.

Order on opposite page

SECOND CHANCE AT LOVE